Advance Praise for *Naturally Powe*

"Out of a cosmology that has endured centuries of human culture and experience, Valerie Wells makes a clear case for personal empowerment in what may well be the ultimate in 'how-to' books. This is a fun and stimulating tutorial on how to get the most out of the way the universe is arranged. It is an exercise and experience guide to the appropriate acquisition and application of *power*. Some Native traditionals I know would call this making good medicine."

—Doug Boyd, author of *Rolling Thunder*

"As the mind/body connection becomes more and more apparent, it is books such as this that help us lovingly make that connection in our lives."

—Harvey Diamond, author of *Fit for Life*

Naturally POWERFUL

200 Simple Actions to Energize Body, Mind, Heart and Spirit

VALERIE WELLS

A Perigee Book

A Perigee Book
Published by The Berkley Publishing Group
A member of Penguin Putnam Inc.
375 Hudson Street
New York, New York 10014

First edition: February 1999

Published simultaneously in Canada.

The Penguin Putnam Inc. World Wide Web site address is
http://www.penguinputnam.com

Library of Congress Cataloging-in-Publication Data

Wells, Valerie.
      Naturally powerful : 200 simple actions to energize body, mind, heart &
spirit / by Valerie Wells. — 1st. ed.
          p.   cm.
      Includes bibliographical references.
      ISBN 0-399-52475-4
      1. Control (Psychology)   2. Control (Psychology)—Problems, exercises,
etc. I. Title.
      BF611.W45   1999
      158—dc21   98-37291
                                                                                      CIP

Printed in the United States of America

10 9 8 7 6 5 4 3 2 1

"Power is the first good."
—Ralph Waldo Emerson

Naturally
POWERFUL

CONTENTS

ACKNOWLEDGMENTS

The process of creating a book, from inception to readers' hands, is all about the power of connection and action that takes place on numerous levels. From my highest heart I thank the Creator, my High Self, and my writing angels for helping me open to the inspiration for this book, and for their energy and guidance in writing it.

Boundless gratitude to my agent, Heide Lange, who is an angel in her own right. Her faith in *Naturally Powerful* gave it wings.

A thousand shining thanks to my editor, Sheila Curry, for her savvy, kindness, and perspicacity.

Mrs. C. and Jim Stuart are my guardian angels here on earth. Their support helped me reconnect with power from which I had become separated, and their prayers enlivened me. I am forever grateful.

On the days when it was difficult to rub two words together and spark a sentence, the bright, loving energy and visualization power of Alan Glines were an inspiration, and precious.

I thank my mother, Anne Blades, for being one of my most powerful teachers.

Very special thanks to Barbara Gibson, Jay Myers, and Brian Jaudon for their expert research and their caring.

I also wish to thank
>   the Finches for their faith in me and their support;
>   writer Christine Bell, whose risk taking encourages me;
>   Betty Rozell for her loving thoughts;
>   Mazie for saying and doing the right thing at the right time;
>   poet Harry Brody, whose kinship with words opens windows in
>   me;
>   Janet and Dominic for being such sweet spirits.

In the talkin' the talk and walkin' the walk department, I want to acknowledge that over the course of writing *Naturally Powerful*, I did every one of the 200 actions set forth, some several times, some every day. They have been gifts in my life.

Power undirected by high purpose spells

calamity; and high purpose by itself is useless

if the power to put it into effect is lacking.

—THEODORE ROOSEVELT

Naturally
POWERFUL

PART I

FINDING YOUR POWER

WHAT IS
POWER?

"**P**OWER is the first good," wrote Ralph Waldo Emerson, because it is essential for achieving every other good. Out of the wellspring of personal power are born loving relationships, success that fulfills, vibrant health, mental agility, financial prosperity, a buoyant sense of well-being, and an enlivening connection with one's spirit.

Power is a force you direct through your actions, which affects you, others, and events. Do you have power? Absolutely! As our birthright and spiritual heritage, each of us is given the potential to be completely powerful, and we spend the rest of our lives discovering our power and learning how to use it constructively.

Like electricity, power itself is neither good nor bad. It is how you use your power that determines its negative or positive impact. People who use their power to manipulate or exploit others give power a bad name. Their actions make it seem as if power is destructive, which can make good-hearted people less inclined to become powerful. The truth is, people who resort to abusing or taking advantage of others are not powerful enough. "Lack of power corrupts absolutely," as statesperson Adlai Stevenson said, although it is often misquoted. People who have developed only a small portion of the power available to them, attempt to make up for their lack of power by either taking other people's power, or preventing them from using it. The power they take is often in the form of money, energy, property, self-esteem, willpower, health, or trust. People who have an abundance of power have neither the need nor the desire to succeed at the expense of others, because they have confidence in their ability to achieve what they want through their own positive actions.

What does it mean to be powerful, or literally, full of power? *Being powerful is the willingness and ability to take constructive action to enhance one's well-being and the well-being of others, now and in the future.*

The cornerstone of the definition is the taking of constructive action. Power is expressed through action. Those who do not act are not powerful. You might have the most brilliant idea for feeding the world's hungry, but if you do not take steps to actualize it, it comes to naught, and you have not been powerful.

To be truly powerful the action must be constructive. Those who act destructively—whether to self, others, or the earth—are not powerful even though they have taken action. While destructive actions have strong impact, their effect is to suppress or negate power.

Constructive means that the action enhances the well-being of all concerned, not just the person initiating the action, or an elite few. If a business transaction increases your profits and those of a handful of investors, but creates hardship or deprivation for others, or injures the earth, you have not acted powerfully. Nor can the gain be positive for the short term, but then turn exploitive down the road. Well-being must be increased not only in the present, but in the future. A truly powerful action does not impede power, but paves the way for future powerful actions.

A naturally powerful person possesses both the willingness and the ability to act positively. If you are aware of the proper course of action but are unwilling to take it, you are not powerful because no action occurs. For example, if you are aware that someone you care about needs help, but you are unwilling to make the effort to help them, you are not being powerful. Nor are you powerful if you are motivated to act, but lack the ability and resources to follow through. If you very much want to help a person in need, but you do not have enough energy, money, connections, or time to do so, your lack of resources prevents you from carrying out your intention and you are unable to be powerful.

Power itself can seem ineffable and elusive because, like the wind, you cannot see it, you can only feel it and see the effects of it. Power may be intangible, but it is very real. Like the wind, power has energy and motion. In physics, power is defined as a system's capacity for doing work, be it an engine or a body. The strength of a system's power is measured according to the amount of energy it emits in a given period of time. The more energy it is capable of expending, the more powerful it is. A 200 horsepower engine is more powerful than a 50 horsepower engine because it can expend four times more energy in the same amount of time. Another key element is that the work must result in accomplishment or it does not qualify as power.

The same principles apply to how powerful you can be. The more energy you are capable of expending in a given period of time, and the more effective the results, the more powerful you are. Where do you find the energy? Physicists have determined that the entire universe is energy. Matter, which appears solid, is actually stored energy moving very slowly. This means that energy is everywhere around you, in the sun, air, water, food, the earth, plants, animals, birds, and insects.

Energy is also within you because you are part of the universe. Your body is composed of decillions of molecules that vibrate and generate energy. Every minute, hundreds of thousands of chemical and electrical activities occur in your brain, generating energy. Your every thought, emotion, word, and action are energy in motion.

In addition to the abundance of energy in nature and within you, spiritual energy is available to you. Your spirit is pure energy as is the Creator. Angels, who are with you whether you believe in them or not, are pure, loving energy, too. In the hierarchy of angels, it is said that the second sphere from the Creator is where the Virtues, Dominions, and Powers dwell. Angels who are Powers have three primary responsibilities: they keep the forces of the universe in balance, they monitor the activities of fallen angels, and they oversee physical life and death.

It is fitting that the main duties of the angels known as Powers directly relate to human beings becoming more powerful. We are a force in the universe. The actions we take cause the energy we expend to be either out of balance or in balance with the universe. The more in harmony our actions are with the universal energy, the more energy we have to use, the more effectively we are able to use it, and the more powerful we are.

The universe is a powerful place and we are meant to be powerful, but we have fallen out of harmony with the grace of the Creator. In a sense we here on earth are fallen angels in training to rise. The further we have distanced ourselves from Ultimate Power, the less powerful we are able to be. It is in acting powerfully on every level—physically, mentally, emotionally, and spiritually—that each of us succeeds in becoming a rising angel.

From the point of view of energy, physical birth and death are powerful events, and it is no wonder that they are overseen by the Powers. These events exemplify the basic law of physics established by Albert Einstein, that energy can neither be created nor destroyed, but it can be transformed. The common example is water which can be a solid, a liquid, or a gas. To our conditioned physical senses, life seems solid and finite, but it is really infinite energy taking different forms. The birth of a baby is the result of our gas-like spiritual energy working to convert energy into liquid and solid forms, connected to the spirit by breath. Death releases the energy that has been stored as matter and returns it to its original spiritual state. Just as a flower draws energy from the earth, sun, rain, air, and gravity, and when it is done, returns the energy to its source, so do our physical bodies. Birth and death are but the life-force transformed.

Every form of energy can be converted into every other form of energy. An engine converts solid or liquid fuel into heat which produces mechanical energy and motion. A nuclear reactor converts atomic energy. A hydroelectric plant converts water energy. To be powerful it is necessary that you connect with some form of energy, whether it is physical, mental, emotional, spiritual, or the energy found in nature, and direct it through action. The higher the quality of energy you use, and the more constructive your actions, the more powerful you are.

If you are looking for a simple formula or a quick fix to become more powerful, there isn't one. Buying an expensive car or taking a pill are artificial devices that create a temporary illusion of power, but actually leave you wandering aimlessly in a state of powerlessness. The more removed an object or an action is from the natural life-force, the less the quantity and quality of its energy, and so the less powerful you are able to be. Objects and actions that have a low-energy level, not only give you less energy with which to work, they lower the quality of your own natural energy, which further limits the effectiveness of your actions. Say for example, that on a scale of one-to-ten your energy vibrates at a level of seven. If you want to achieve ten of something, but engage in actions that have energy levels of three, you will be lucky to achieve five. Or think of it as trying to build a one story 3,000-square-foot house in a 1,000-square-foot lot; your actions are limited by the boundaries of the energy with which you surround yourself.

Power is the life-force given to you by the Creator to help you learn, grow, love, and create. The adventure of discovering authentic power begins inside you, with the emphasis being on the journey not the destination. According to an ancient Chinese saying, "A thousand mile journey begins with a single step." Without taking the action of the single step, there is no journey, no discovery, no adventure, no power. The journey to empowerment, however, does not take place along a straight path, but unfolds in all directions, all at once. The paths to power are shaped more like a spoked wheel. *Naturally Powerful* gets you rolling with 200 energizing steps that connect you with the natural power of your body, mind, heart, spirit, relationships, nature, and the power of the Creator.

Knowing how to join forces with the energy within you and

around you, empowers you to take charge of your thoughts, feelings, words, and actions, which in turn empowers you to take charge of your life. Natural power becomes both the tool and the material necessary to craft your life in ways that bring you comfort, aliveness, fulfillment, and joy.

MORE

POWER

NEEDED

LIKE having electricity, or an engine in your car, you need power to operate your life. Without it you can be left in the dark, you don't move forward, and living your life is much more difficult. This is true on physical, mental, emotional, and spiritual levels.

If you have become disconnected from power, or have lost what it takes to turn it on, your life will let you know. Here are some of the conditions that signal the need to plug into power:

- · Unable to create the resources and opportunities you need
- · Relationships are fraught with conflict
- · Chronic illness
- · Waking up feeling apprehensive and tense
- · A sense of being overwhelmed by life
- · Often feeling sad, unhappy, or depressed
- · Struggling to achieve your goals
- · Being disappointed by people
- · Not having as much love as you want
- · Being angry with people, situations, and life
- · Feeling separate and alienated

Not only do you need power to turn these conditions around, but you are living in a time when life is becoming more accelerated and condensed, which creates an even greater need for power. The events you experience in a day might have taken two weeks to transpire a hundred years ago. A process that might have taken a year to unfold then, might take two months now. The centrifugal force produced by this acceleration is causing people and events to spin away from their centers and out to extremes. Duality is already an intrinsic part of life on earth, where just about everything has its opposite—day/night, love/hate, positive/negative—but the increased rate of the speed of life is producing even more profound diametric effects.

For example, the rapid changes taking place in the fields of communication and technology are polarizing people around the globe into those who have access to information and those who do not. Economic changes are polarizing people into those who have money to buy food, shelter, health, freedom, tools, and security, and those who do not have enough money to cover basic necessities.

The effects of polarization apply not only to material assets, but to mental, emotional, and spiritual assets as well. Some people are becoming more intelligent, and others are becoming less intelligent. Some people are becoming more loving, others are becoming more angry. Some people are becoming more sensitive, others are becoming more obtuse. Some people are becoming more connected to the Creator, and others are becoming more separated. However, it is possible that this intense polarization is a prelude to greater harmony, the dark before the dawn.

Although we tend to regard the Earth only as a planet, it has a body, a consciousness, a heart, and a spirit, just as we do. The Earth too is changing. The shifts taking place in the geology, energy, and spirit of the Earth reflect the changes taking place in humankind and also empower them. Like a snake that sheds its old skin as it grows, the Earth and the lives she nourishes are sloughing off old systems of thinking, doing, and being, to make way for new, expanded, more evolved systems.

Because all energy is interconnected and our mental and emotional energy affects the energy of the Earth, resisting the changes due to fear could make the transformations taking place more severe. Fear also creates discord because it causes separation from power. A better strategy is to become attuned to the higher loving frequencies of energy being generated by the Earth. This requires connecting with higher quality energy, and raising the quality of your actions on every level.

Those who give their power away to gloom and doom could create the very experiences they fear, but those who embrace and express their true power can experience transcendent changes in consciousness. It is as if the world itself is issuing a mandate: To successfully meet the complex challenges of life now and in the future, people must become the powerful beings they are meant to be. Without the power to act constructively a great deal can be lost, or not attained.

These dramatic changes have set in motion a spiritual revolution that is impelling people to seek a balance between their material and spiritual natures. The new millennium, too, is motivating people to re-evaluate their lives, making them more inclined to put their material well-being in perspective as providing support for the spiritual quest, for it is from the spiritual realm that all true power comes.

THREE

POWERFUL

BENEFITS

Genuine power enriches every aspect of your life on every level. Power is to you as electricity is to your life. It illuminates your path so you can see your way more clearly, with less stumbling and falling. It provides energy you can plug into to do whatever you want or need to do, and do it more easily. When you are connected to your power you are able to manifest the love, vibrant health, abundant material resources, fulfilling relationships, and success you desire.

When you are physically powerful, for example, your body is fit, well coordinated, and well-nourished, and you are able to easily and efficiently accomplish physical activities. You have achieved such overall physical strength because you have exercised your whole body and provided it with healthy, high energy fuel. If you were to exercise only your left leg and right arm, other key areas would be undeveloped and weak, causing your body to function improperly and inefficiently. If you were to feed your body unhealthy food with little nutritional value, you would feel tired and lack energy.

The same principles apply to the four dimensions of your being— body, mind, heart, and spirit—which are simply different parts of the same system, just as the different parts of your body belong to the same physical system. If you are exercising your mind but not your spirit, your whole system becomes out of kilter and cannot function effectively. If you nourish your body but starve your emotions, you will not have the energy you need to be completely successful. You have probably noticed people whose systems are not healthy and in harmony, and so are disconnected from their power. They look tired and gray, and their eyes are lifeless. Powerful people glow with the energy of well-being and their eyes are bright and lively. Taking healthy, constructive, nourishing action in all dimensions of your being produces overall health, vitality, efficiency, effectiveness, and strength, which in turn produces more energy and power.

The actions in *Naturally Powerful* are designed to exercise the major muscle groups of your physical, mental, emotional, and spiritual bodies, making them strong and balanced so they can function in unison. Such a holistic approach creates a natural synergy of powerfulness. The actions also provide you with the raw material you need to be powerful, and the tools for getting your power in shape. Some of the benefits you might experience are:

Enhanced self-image
Raised success consciousness
Clearer thinking
Improved communication skills
Improved ability to manage emotions
Reduced stress
Ability to take risks that further growth
Stronger positive intention
Respect for the body in which you live
Respect for the planet on which you live
Deeper compassion
Revived intuition
Willingness to make ethical choices
Being more responsible
Increased creativity
Being a better problem-solver
Expanded awareness of self, others, your world, and the Creator

Acting powerfully on all levels, in all areas of your life, enables you to harness energy to work for you. It also generates more energy that you can use to become more powerful. The energy you generate benefits not only you as an individual, but others. Energy is dynamic, not stationary, so your vibrant, healthy, clear, focused energy ripples out, uplifting those around you. Marianne Williamson said, "Our deepest fear is not that we are inadequate, our deepest fear is that we are powerful beyond measure. . . . As we are liberated from our own fear, our presence automatically liberates others."

USING
THIS
BOOK

WHEN you use any part of this book in any way, you are being powerful, because you are taking constructive action that enhances well-being. Even if you were to use this book to press autumn leaves, or as a coaster for a glass of sparkling water, you would in a sense be using it powerfully. Of course there are more powerful ways to benefit from *Naturally Powerful*. Understanding the format and being aware of different ways to read it, will help you use the book to good effect.

FORMAT

Combining high level energy and action increases the strength of your power. Each of the 200 one-page actions describes a positive activity that connects you to a physical, mental, emotional, or spiritual energy, and defines the benefits of taking the action. If energy tends to become blocked on a particular level, those symptoms and their consequences are identified, as well as which actions are needed to get the energy flowing. If there are powerful times and places for carrying out the activity, or special materials that are required, such information is also included.

Two-hundred actions was settled on as being a generous, but not overwhelming number of entries. Having a diversity of actions gives you plenty of latitude to choose the ones that work best for you. Limiting each chapter to a single page helps make the information more accessible, and allows you—especially if you're busy, or suffering from information overload—to easily sample a variety of selections.

A suggested action might be primarily physical, mental, emotional, or spiritual in nature, but it will affect all four dimensions because they are all interconnected. To reflect the interconnection of energy, a chapter that focuses on energizing your body might be right next to one that energizes your spirit. Your analytical, linear left brain would undoubtedly prefer to have the chapters logically arranged in categories, but that format could inhibit you from experiencing the wonderful world of your right brain. Although left-brain thinking has many practical uses, verbal and math skills among them, it is the right brain that is creative, intuitive, and holistic. The right brain is also the gateway to the wealth of information in your subconscious mind, as well as the wisdom and compassion of your supraconscious mind. To keep the subject matter of the chapters separate would contradict the very nature of power, which is synergistic; it combines energy from different sources to produce greater results than any singular source of energy would yield. Like a deck of 200 playing cards, the actions are shuffled together to both reflect and encourage the integration of the four suits of life: body, mind, heart, and spirit.

Mixing up the topics also gives people who tend to focus on one particular area, opportunities to engage in other types of activities. You cannot expect to be a powerful person if you are physically fit, but spiritually underdeveloped, or are a whiz at math, but inept at connecting emotionally with people. Being truly powerful means being willing and able to act effectively in every facet of your life, in thought, word, and deed.

Each one-page action is like a blueprint for a building. It outlines the basic shape and style of the action to take, but you are the one who actually builds the house. Feel free to modify the design to accommodate your particular needs and preferences. To learn more about a particular subject, and further expand your power in that area, refer to the books listed in the bibliography. Talking with people who are knowledgeable about the areas in which you are interested is also enriching and stimulating.

The spectrum of activities in *Naturally Powerful* provides tools and materials necessary for building power. They are natural in that they can be done using what is readily available in your environment, in nature, and within you. Many of the actions require no material resources at all, but simply suggest what to do, think, say, or feel, either by yourself, or with others. (You might want to keep a notebook to write in for some of the exercises).

When referring to The Force that Creates Everything and Is Alive in Everything, I use the name Creator. It is simple, active, and universal, and it is not gender specific. Although the Creator embraces both masculine and feminine energy, It is much, much more. Our language does not have a pronoun that accurately expresses what the Creator is. Being both a he and a she, and yet neither, the only remaining pronoun to use is It. Because of our limited thinking, we tend to think of an it as an inanimate object. But all matter is energy, and all energy has consciousness given to it by the Creator, so referring to the Creator as an It becomes the most appropriate solution. That said, feel free to call the Creative Force by any name you want and use any pronoun, because the Creator is not changed by what you call it. A name simply gives you a way to refer to It and connect with It. The Creator is the Creator is the Creator, regardless.

USING THE BOOK

In keeping with the spirit of *Naturally Powerful*, you have the power to choose to do any activity at any time you want. You can read through the book from front to back in orderly left-brain fashion, or you can do it the right brain way and be spontaneous.

Try scanning the table of contents, letting a word or a phrase in a title pique your interest. Your subconscious and supraconscious minds already know every word and every comma on every page, before you even crack open the cover, so let them guide you to the chapter that would be most beneficial for you. To connect with your intuitive knowledge, hold the book, close your eyes, take a few deep breaths, and open the book at random, letting your finger point to one of the two actions on the facing pages. Or before you open the book, choose the left or right hand page.

Which action, or when it is done, is not so important as *that* it is done. Each positive step taken, whether large or small, activates and amplifies power. Some actions will not appeal to you at all, or you will feel they relate to areas in which you are already proficient. That's fine, don't do them. The purpose of the variety of chapters is to give you plenty of latitude. Some chapters that seem boring or irrelevant now, may become interesting a year or five years from now, or never hold your interest. You may try some actions once and not want to do them again. That's fine, too. Becoming more powerful is not furthered by putting pressure on yourself. You may be drawn to do some of the actions several times, and a few special ones will light up your life so effectively that you may choose to do them every day.

Being powerful is connecting with the energy of your body, mind, heart, and spirit, and the energy of nature and the Creator, and using that energy to take actions that further you and others. If you only do one action offered in *Naturally Powerful*, or even one part of one action, you will increase the strength of your power.

The power of a man is his present means

to obtain some future apparent good.

—THOMAS HOBBES

·

Lack of power corrupts absolutely.

—ADLAI STEVENSON

PART II

200 SIMPLE ACTIONS TO ENERGIZE BODY, MIND, HEART, AND SPIRIT

GREETING THE DAY

Each new day holds in its arms gifts of opportunity, learning, adventure, and fulfillment. By greeting the day with thankfulness every morning, you prepare the way for receiving its gifts. Respectful acknowledgment of the day helps you be more alert to possibilities for love, learning, and success. It also raises your energy level so you attract more positive people and experiences.

Create a special ritual for greeting the day. It can be as simple as facing east, where the sun rises, and saying, "Thank you for this day." Or from the east, turn sunward to your right, honoring the four directions. Light a symbolic candle. Meditate on what you want to accomplish during the day. Say prayers.

Ask for guidance from the higher force with which you feel connected: God, Goddess, Creator, al-Lah, Yahweh, Jesus Christ, Buddha, Abraham, Virgin Mary, Mohammed, Brahma, Great Spirit, Lao Zi, Angels, Archangels, Isis, Jah, Kwan-yin, or Zeus. Or devise a name that has meaning for you. The name is not as important as being in touch with the force itself. As Shakespeare wrote in *Romeo and Juliet,* "The rose by any other name would smell as sweet."

You can create a personal greeting to the day, or try this one:

A new day has begun,
I greet the earth, the sun, the seas, the sky,
And all who walk and crawl and swim and fly,
May we all live in loving harmony as one.
Sacred Creator,
Please guide me, and guard me, and gift me today,
Lift my heart and light my way
In all that I think, and feel, and do, and say.
Thank you for this day and its gift of light,
Enliven it with love, success, and delight.

BEGINNINGS

B EGINNINGS are vitally important. The quality of action with which you begin something—a job, a journey, or a relationship—often determines the quality of everything that follows.

The process of beginning is similar to laying a foundation for a house: you need strong, enduring materials, and the size and shape must take into account what it is to support. If any part of the foundation is weak or out of alignment, the structure you try to build will be askew and could topple altogether.

The layout of your beginning comes from your intention, which means plan or design. Write an outline or draw a blueprint of your goals before undertaking physical action. What kinds of experiences do you want to house and shelter? What windows of opportunity do you want to open? What doors of learning do you want to walk through? What people and ideas do you want to entertain? To create the best plan for your future, be honest and practical about your goals.

Once you're clear about the shape and size of your goals, you gain a better idea of what to do to accomplish them. Your initial actions become the materials that make up the foundation. It is their strength and integrity that endures. Write down what you need to do to create the best experiences for yourself and others. Ask for help from those involved and from your Creator.

Taking ten minutes at the start of a new endeavor to define what you want to accomplish and how to do it, can save you days, weeks, months, or even years of headaches, heartaches, and money aches down the road. Clear, strong plans and actions at the beginning, support and empower your future.

JUMP-STARTING POWER

To quote songwriter Bob Dylan, "The times they are a-changin'." And because they are changing so quickly—economically, politically, socially, and geophysically—the times they are a-challengin'. You need all the natural power you can muster to survive, and also to thrive.

Jump-start your power when you first wake up, before distractions set in. While still in bed, lie on your back and place your hands on either side of your abdomen as if holding a bowl. The Chinese believe that the center of gravity for your life force, or *chi*, is in your belly. This chi energy provides physical, mental, emotional, and spiritual strength, stability, and health. Chi also means breath because the Chinese view energy and breath as one in the same. Encircling your abdomen with your hands helps you focus on your chi, and also on your abdominal muscles, which assist you in breathing.

Even though you breathe primarily with your lungs, it is possible to direct the energy of your breath into other parts of your body. With your hands around the sides of your abdomen, breathe in all the way down into the bottom of your belly. Imagine that you are pouring energy into your belly bowl, filling it up. You might sense the energy as liquid light. When you exhale, imagine that you are releasing tensions and toxins, both physical and emotional.

With each breath cycle say silently or aloud, "I am naturally powerful." About four deep breaths and affirmations are usually all that's needed to give you calm, centered, powerful energy to effectively handle the events that lie ahead. Nourishing yourself with power is as vital as eating nourishing food. Fill your belly bowl with breath and you'll get your get-up-and-go going.

4

LOVE LESSONS

HAVE you ever felt afraid of another person, an upcoming event, or your feelings? Has a situation or a person ever made you feel angry? Have you ever felt sad about something that happened? If you are human and even minimally self-aware, you probably answered yes at least once.

When you feel frightened, angry, or sad, you tend to feel far removed from love, but you are closer than you think. The Creator, your higher self which has a wide and wise overview of your life purposes, and your guardian angel love you beyond measure, and They want you to be the most loveful, joyful, powerful being you can be. One way They help you fulfill your potential is by connecting you to events that connect you with emotions stored within you that block you from loving yourself, others, the planet, the universe, or Them. The "soul" purpose of these events is to trigger and release the emotions—whether from adulthood, adolescence, childhood, or even infancy—that come between you and love.

Events that produce disagreeable feelings will continue to occur until the emotional blocks are released and replaced with love. The healthy release of emotions is addressed in other chapters, the emphasis here is on the advantage of attitude. View difficult emotions, events, and people from the perspective that they are Divinely inspired for the purpose of healing and growth. Such objectivity strengthens you and increases your compassion for yourself and others. Instead of feeling powerless, or as if you were being punished, understanding the loving intent behind challenging events better equips you to take charge of them.

Keep in mind and heart that the goal of life experiences is to teach you love of all that exists and it will help you heal obstacles and move closer to love.

HOME SACRARIUM

A sacrarium is a sanctuary or shrine where you can focus your thoughts, calm your emotions, center and increase energy, and receive knowledge and healing. It is a sacred place for connecting with yourself and your Creator so you can better fulfill both your worldly and spiritual aspirations.

To create a sacrarium in your home, set aside an area that can be made private and quiet. It might be an entire room, a nook set apart by a folding screen, a closet, or even a shelf. Provide a comfortable place to sit, be it a chair or a pillow on the floor. Choose clear colors—rather than dark or muddy—that uplift.

You will also need a table or shelf that is at a height in proportion to your seating arrangements. It is preferable if it is made out of wood or other natural material, but any flat surface will do. Place something of the earth on it, such as a shell, leaf, crystal, stone, flower, or something metal. Also place on the table, incense, fresh water, and a candle which can burn safely so all four elements are represented. Include objects that are spiritually powerful for you: a special piece of jewelry, a ceremonial sword, a moving prayer or poem, pictures of inspiring spiritual or world leaders, photos of loved ones, a photo of you being happy, pictures of goals you want to achieve, stimulating colors, and so forth.

It is well worth your while to spend at least a few minutes in your sacrarium every day. It is a place where, as American philosopher Joseph Campbell said, "creative incubation" can occur. Be aware of your breathing. Call in the light. Define your goals. Say a prayer. Ask for healing, guidance, and protection. Be one with peace. Talk to your supraconscious, your angels, the Creator. Listen.

MONEY BLESSINGS

MONEY is perceived as many things—power, status, success—but at its most elementary level it is really just a convenient symbol for energy. To acquire money you have to expend physical, mental, emotional, or spiritual energy. The value of those actions is translated into a dollar amount by you or someone else, and the appropriate amount of money is exchanged.

Like electricity and power, money itself is neither negative nor positive; it is how you use money that determines the effect it has on you and others. To clear, uplift, and expand the energy of money, bless it. *Webster's Dictionary* defines *to bless* as: "to invoke divine care for; praise, glorify; to speak gratefully of; to confer prosperity or happiness upon." The steps of the following blessing ritual evoke these principles (use your own heartfelt words):

- Hold the cash or check with both hands so that the positive and negative, masculine and feminine poles of your energy are in contact with it, energizing it.
- Visualize a ball of white light surrounding the money or check. This clears any negative energy attached to it.
- Give thanks to the Creator for helping you to receive the money.
- Give thanks to yourself for taking action to receive it.
- Combine your energy with the Creator's to uplift, expand and magnetize the money. See the money as a magnet that attracts more money to you.
- Ask that the person who gave you the money be blessed with ten times the energy of the money they gave you, in the form for which they most have need, with your gratitude.

No matter how much or how little money you have, receiving money is a blessing. Conferring light and happiness on money assures future blessings.

KNOWING SELF

P OET Rainer Maria Rilke wrote, "Who's not sat tense before his own heart's curtain?" It is a dramatic and accurate image because too often we are reluctant to attend our true hearts for fear of seeing a horror show. Yet not knowing yourself puts you at a severe disadvantage when it comes to knowing how best to act in the ever-changing scenarios life stages.

An easy, but effective way to increase your knowledge of yourself, and so increase your power to act constructively, is to spontaneously complete the following ten lines with words from your heart and mind. Do not critique them. Write your insights here or on a separate sheet of paper. It is helpful to do these lines repeatedly, once a week or once a month. Observing how the dialogue changes or stays the same shines light upon the nature of your character.

I need _____
I want _____
I think _____
I believe _____
I feel _____
I secretly _____
I fear _____
I need to prove _____
I am _____
I will _____

• ⌒ •

Knowing your lines by heart helps you perform well upon the stages of life.

ANGEL COUNTRY

You have probably heard that every person on the planet—including you—has a guardian angel who watches over them. When you are experiencing a crisis, whether you are awash in pain, burning up with fever, or in conflict with yourself or others, you can call upon your guardian angel for help.

Each country in the world also has a guardian angel, known as a principality, watching over the land, its people, and its leaders. When there is a crisis—floods, fires, famines, war—call upon the guardian angel of the country for help. You don't have to live in that country to request the angel's assistance, nor do you have to know the angel's name. You only need to ask.

Angels respect the free-will given to us by our Creator, so they do not intervene until we ask them to, except in extreme circumstances that would hinder our growth rather than further it. When you appeal to an angel to help the country they oversee, your prayer goes directly from your heart to the heart of the angel. Once angels receive permission to act, they gather and direct the energy of the Creator, and all the prayers sent, to provide healing, support, guidance, protection, and miracles for the people and the earth. The more prayers, the more help given.

You can petition the country's angel through formal prayer, or by simply speaking from your heart. It always helps raise energy levels to ask that the troubled area and all its inhabitants be filled and surrounded with harmonizing light. You may also ask that the land be healed, a leader be guided, people be protected, or whatever specific request is appropriate. At the end of your petition it is essential that you entrust everything to the wisdom of the Creator, saying, "May that which is for the highest good of all life forms be done."

GOOD FOR BAD

JUST about everyone becomes angry at someone sometime, but anger usually flares up and burns itself out. If you find yourself constantly refueling the anger by replaying the offending incident over and over again in your mind, you turn anger into resentment. Over time the resentment becomes toxic, poisoning your physical, mental, emotional, and spiritual systems. You might become sick, pessimistic, chronically unhappy, or cynical about the Creator. The degree of distress you experience is often in direct proportion to the degree of your resentment.

The consequences of resentment are simply not worth the effort of keeping it going. One way to break the destructive loop of resentment in which you are caught, is to wish for good things to happen to the person you resent.

Once you've picked yourself up off the floor from the shock of such a thought, consider trying it. Sit comfortably. Breathe deeply a few times. Imagine yourself in a beautiful place outdoors. Visualize the person you resent being happy, healthy, prosperous, or whatever condition you know they need.

The first thing that happens is that you cannot imagine anything nice happening to someone who was anything but nice to you. Nobody said this would be easy. Keep trying. Your feelings of resentment will intensify. This is a good thing; it means your intention is prying up your resentment. Try again. You feel as angry as you did initially. Let go of the loosened angry energy, but do no harm. Yell. Bang pots. Run. Replace the angry image with a friendly image.

When you succeed in wishing the person well, you will feel noticeably lighter, calmer, and stronger. This is because you have freed your energy from the snare of resentment, and you can now use the energy to take positive action.

PERSONAL COUNCIL

CHOICES come in all shapes and sizes. So do decisions. Each decision we make, whether large or small, defines who we are and the quality of person we are becoming. The very act of making a decision is empowering. Even if it later becomes apparent that it was not the best decision, you have a better chance of succeeding if you set things in motion, rather than remaining static.

To improve your chances of making good decisions, establish a personal council of valued friends. Consult them when you are faced with major decisions regarding career, relationships, finances, large purchases, or where to live.

Begin by making a list of the people to whom you feel the closest. From this master list choose from three to seven people whose perceptions you trust and who have well-developed communication skills. It increases the quality of input you receive if both genders are represented in balanced numbers.

To the extent possible, the members of the council should share among them a diversity of skills, such as an understanding of human behavior, legal expertise, and financial acumen. The single most important characteristic that all should share is a deep and abiding caring for your well-being.

Write or call each person whom you select to invite them to be part of your personal council. Explain its function. If logistically possible, meet in person whenever you have an issue before you that you want to discuss. Otherwise, you can contact each council member individually and sound them out.

Ultimately, the decision is yours alone, but the perspectives and feedback you gain from others can be invaluable in helping you arrive at a decision that furthers you.

LEFT TO RIGHT

WHERE does your conscious mind spend the most time? On the left or right side of your brain?

Your brain has two hemispheres, a left and a right. The two sides are connected by a bridge of nerve fibers called the *corpus callosum*, which allows information to pass back and forth between the two halves. The left hemisphere processes words and numbers, analyzes, views time and space as being linear and sequential, and is logical and objective. The right hemisphere processes emotions, imagines, views time and space as being whole and circular, and is intuitive and subjective. From the Chinese perspective, the left brain is *yang* or masculine, and the right is *yin* or feminine. In our technological society, left-brain activities tend to be favored over right.

When you talk, read, write, crunch numbers, analyze, watch the clock, deduce, put things in order, and are right-handed, your left brain is active. When you draw, design structures, dream, daydream, follow your instincts, forget time, experience spontaneous insights, sense how another person is feeling, feel close to nature, and are left-handed, your right brain is active.

As with many aspects of life, balance is key. If you spend most of your time in your left-brain, take a trip across the bridge to your right brain where new adventures await you. You might even discover a creative solution to a problem. Engage in right brain activities. Be aware of each breath. Do not count them. Sense what you are feeling. Do not rationalize it. Take photographs. Do not critique them. Use your left hand to draw or sculpt. Do not write. You're right in your right mind.

STAND UP FOR YOUR FEET

EVERYTHING rests upon your feet. They support you, provide balance, and move you forward. They link you to the earth. If your body were a building, your feet would be the foundation. Your feet are essential, but other than putting shoes on them, most people do not give their feet the attention they deserve.

It is time to stand up for your feet. Treat your feet in the manner to which they would like to become accustomed. Choose shoes that are comfortable and supportive. Soak your feet in a warm bath of Epsom salts to dissolve tension and aches. Keep your toenails trimmed straight across to help prevent ingrown toenails. Use your hands to stretch your toes forward and back. Before going to bed, massage your feet with oil or lotion. Visit a podiatrist.

Reflexologists respect feet from an even more comprehensive perspective. They see each foot as a homunculus, meaning that each foot is like a little person with all the major parts of the body represented. By massaging specific points correlating to particular points of the body, you increase and balance energy flow in those areas and improve your health. For example: toes are believed to correspond to the head, the tips to the sinuses; the soles reflect internal organs, the stomach point being on the ball of the foot beneath the big toe, and the heart point being under the little toe just below the ball of the foot.

The foot may also have psychological connections, its flexibility relating to your flexibility as a person. The heel relates to the mother, the first joint of the big toe to the father. Flat feet may indicate a collapse of energy, corns may indicate conflict.

Care for your feet well so that each foot you put forward is your best.

PRAYER POWER

THROUGHOUT the world, prayer is probably the most often practiced religious ritual, but you do not have to be religious to practice it. Praying is really a spiritual experience, an intimate conversation between you and the loving, wise higher force you acknowledge and respect. The name you call this universal energy is up to you. This higher force exists within you and everywhere, allowing you to pray anywhere—temple, church, home, hospital, prison, meadow, or sea.

Prayer can be used to praise, express gratitude, and affirm faith, but is probably most often used to petition for help for yourself or others. The help requested could be for healing, guidance, resources, strength, forgiveness, humility, understanding, protection, comfort, or love. Use words from prayers you know, or your own special words, but always pray from your heart. The sincerity of your words is what helps them shine and gives them wings.

Do not specify what form the help is to take because it restricts the ways in which assistance can come to you and inhibits the manifestation of miracles. The higher forces have a bigger picture of your life and its purposes than you do. At the end of a prayer, ask that the will of the omniscient force you pray to—not yours—be done. This sets the prayer free. Prayer works. Cardiac patients who were prayed for by strangers did better than those who were not prayed for.

Assume a posture that keeps your spine straight so your energy can flow freely. Like batteries, our bodies are storehouses of energy, with the left and right hands like negative and positive terminals. Putting the palms of your hands together in front of your heart completes a natural vital circuit and directs the energy of your prayer from your heart out and up to the angels and the Creator.

THEN AND NOW

How was your childhood? There were bound to have been both good times and not so good times, perhaps even painful times, but in general what adjectives and phrases would you use to describe it? How did your parents treat you? What emotions did you feel most often? Did you feel safe? What did you like to do? Did you play mostly by yourself or with other children?

At the head of a sheet of paper write, "Childhood." Make a list of answers to the above questions, and any others that occur to you. Avoid complicated or fancy answers, just jot down clear, concise words and phrases.

How is your adulthood? Are you having more good times or bad times? In general, what adjectives and phrases would you use to describe it? How do people treat you? What emotions do you feel most often? Do you feel safe? What do you like to do? Do you play? By yourself or with others?

On a separate sheet of paper write, "Adulthood." Make a list of your answers, putting them in the same order as your "Childhood" answers.

Put the two sheets of paper side by side, "Childhood" on the left and "Adulthood" on the right. How do your two sets of responses compare? Which answers are similar? Which are different? What surprises you? Is there something you liked to do as a child that you have neglected as an adult? Have you changed negative childhood patterns, or are you repeating them? How have your patterns of play changed or stayed the same? Do the people with whom you interact treat you the same way your parents did, or differently?

Seeing the similarities and differences between your childhood and adulthood reveal what to congratulate yourself on, and what you want to change.

SPINNING FOR JOY

WHENEVER you are feeling a quart low on energy, try spinning clockwise. By turning in the same direction as the sun's light moves around the Earth, you create a kind of vortex that pulls positive energy to you. Here's how to put the best spin on spinning.

Pick an open area indoors or outdoors where you won't bump into anything. Stand facing east, then turn smoothly to your right, which will be south, then to the west and north, and back to east. Repeat. You are spinning. Spin on. If your arms want to naturally rise up and out from your sides, let them.

You might feel a bit awkward for the first few spins, but as you continue you will notice that your whirling begins to flow smoothly. You will feel more alive and energized, more in harmony with yourself and the spinning earth. Feeling a bit dizzy is part of the fun and the whirl of energy, but if you are uncomfortable feeling that way, use the trick ballet dancers and ice skaters use when they spin. Pick out an object at eye level, and focus on it as you flash past it each time you complete a turn. It helps stabilize you.

Making a sound while you spin also helps you focus. A sound might just flow from you, or you can repeat a positive or sacred word. This also raises your energy level and helps you connect with the universal spirit.

Spinning is not a new idea. The Sufis of the Middle East have a strong and long tradition of whirling, as do several native tribes throughout the world.

Spin clockwise anytime you want more energy. Spin in the morning to wake you up and align your energy. Spin in the afternoon as a picker-upper. Spin just for fun. Spin for harmony. Spin for joy.

REVERSE SPIN

FEELING wound up? Restless? Or is your mind racing at ninety miles an hour, but your body feels as if it is crawling along well under the speed limit? Try spinning counterclockwise to equalize your energy and unwind.

If spinning clockwise makes you feel energized, then it makes sense that spinning in the opposite direction will make you feel sleepy. Have you ever noticed how much easier it is to travel toward the west than the east? When you move in the direction the sun takes around the earth, you arrive feeling rested, even refreshed. When you travel counter to the path of the sun, you feel like a salmon swimming upstream. Instead of arriving feeling rested, you arrive feeling in need of rest.

Think of spinning counterclockwise like unwinding a yo-yo. The string and yo-yo remain connected, but the momentum of movement temporarily ceases and tension is released. To unwind your string, stand in an area in your home where there is enough space to spin without bumping into anything. Face west, then turn towards your left to the south, then east, and north. As you continue spinning to your left, you unwind.

It is advisable to be dressed for bed before spinning counterclockwise, because it usually does not take too long before you are able to fall asleep. Even as you spin you will feel restlessness settle down, and your mind will float as if upon a calm sea.

The next morning, if you are feeling not quite awake, get your get-up-and-go going by spinning clockwise with the sun. Spinning works both ways!

ANCIENT HEALING

This powerful healing technique has been passed down through generations of Native Americans. It cleanses energy congestion on physical, mental, emotional, and spiritual levels, and it enhances vitality. The treatments are done with a partner, allowing each of you to give and receive healing. A treatment takes from three to five minutes, and must be repeated once on each of five consecutive days.

When you are doing the healing, stand behind the person who should also be standing. Ask the light to fill and surround you and the healee and to guide you. Place your left hand gently around the person's forehead to keep their head from falling forward, and place your right hand at the base of the person's spine. Using the soft pad or side of your thumb, gently slide your thumb along the sides of the person's spine, alternating left and right sides in short, quick strokes. When you reach the top of the spine, use both hands to gently massage their neck and shoulders, again with quick strokes. Using your fingertips, lightly brush down their arms and back with many rapid strokes. It also helps for the healee to visualize themselves being healthy and happy.

When you receive the first healing, you might feel rushes of warm energy in the areas of your body where energy is needed or was blocked. The healing energy might give you goosebumps or chills, or it might make you tingle. You will feel energized for a time, and then you may feel tired as the physical, mental, and emotional toxins and tensions begin to be released. This could be especially apparent after the second day's treatment. After the fifth day you will feel significantly stronger, clearer, brighter, and more optimistic. Welcome health!

SEEDS OF SUCCESS

WHERE does success begin? Think about it. What answer first leaps to mind? If you said your mind, you'd be right. It is the idea of a specific success that occurs first. That idea, like a seed, blossoms best when it contains all the information about what the success looks like and when it's supposed to bloom.

As soon as conception of success occurs, begin to define and refine it. Create a clear and complete mental picture of yourself achieving your ideal success—the flower of your success already in full bloom. What kind of setting are you in? Indoors or outdoors? What style clothes are you wearing? Make sure that at least one item of clothing is in your favorite color. Are other people present? Picture them there. What activity is taking place? What sounds do you hear? What aromas do you smell? What is the temperature of the air?

How long will it take this success to grow to maturity? A month? A year? Be realistic. For instance, if you tell your subconscious that you want to lose twenty pounds by tomorrow, your disbelief could sabotage any weight loss at any time. Pick a month and year for your success to bloom, then insert them clearly into the picture in a calendar or a newspaper, or create a colorful banner with the month (spelled out) and the year emblazoned on it.

Once the seed of your success is fully formed, it is automatically planted in your subconscious mind. Your subconscious becomes like the earth, supporting your success and supplying nutrients for its growth. Shine the light of your intention and attention upon your goal and water it with positive physical action. These steps help all your seeds of success bear delicious, nutritious fruit!

TO A TEE

The hand with which you write is strongly connected to your brain, which means that not only what you write, but how you write it, conveys information to your subconscious mind. In longhand, write the following sentence: "Thanking the Creator suits me to a tee." Did you cross each letter tee from right to left, or left to right? If you're not sure, write the sentence again and check.

When you cross your tees from right to left you are telling your subconscious that you want to stay focused on the past. It then helps you do that because it is supposed to support your thoughts and actions. The problem is that by focusing primarily on the past and not on the future, your future becomes blurry. And because the future is always becoming the present, your daily experiences become a blur and your successes are sketchy. The message you give your subconscious to focus on the past may be so strong that you find it difficult to look at the future.

You can help shift your focus by changing the direction of how you cross your tees. Crossing every tee from left to right tells your subconscious that you want to focus on your future. Write the sentence again: "Thanking the Creator suits me to a tee." At first you will probably cross some of your tees right to left out of habit, but each time you do, go back and re-cross them from left to right. Your subconscious will get the new message.

Changing direction to left-to-right may take a few days, even a week, but you will notice that not only is it easier to look at your future, you want to. As you gladly think about how you want your future to be, your present and your successes become vibrantly alive. Your life suits you to a tee!

IT'S A TREAT

ARE you always on the go? From the moment you open your eyes until you close them, are you busy attending meetings, helping others, taking care of family, picking people up, dropping them off, cooking meals, rushing hither and yon, shopping, making phone calls, having repairs made, meeting deadlines?

Other than when you are sleeping, how much time do you spend in twenty-four hours doing something, anything for yourself? Two hours? One hour? Twenty minutes? No minutes?

If you answered no minutes, chances are you are running on empty. If you said twenty minutes, you probably have about a quart of fuel sloshing around in your tank. How far can you go on little or no fuel? This rhetorical question emphasizes how essential it is to pump energy into yourself on a regular basis. If the Creator cares about you enough to give you life, then out of respect it behooves you to care about yourself. And the better you care for yourself, the more fully you can care for others. If you try to give to others when you yourself are empty, you end up resenting the very people to whom you want to give.

Put your name on one hour out of every twenty-four. Do something that delights you. Give yourself high octane attention. Have a massage. Play tennis. Meditate. Go somewhere special for lunch. Visit a museum. Take a hike. If owning an hour of the day is simply too much, give yourself half an hour. Once a week spend half a day, or longer, doing exactly what you want to do, when you want to do it. Play golf. Stay in bed and read. Go to a movie. Do nothing. Take time to be with yourself, just thinking and feeling. Breathe deeply.

Treating yourself well is a treat to your body, mind, and spirit.

THE PRESENT PRESENT

How often are you doing one thing and thinking about another? Maybe you are at work on Monday morning, but you are thinking about the great time you had over the weekend. Or your child is telling you what happened in school today, and you're wondering what you're going to serve for dinner.

If you spend more time hoping something will hurry up and be over, or thinking about the past or the future instead of being fully aware of the present, you are diminishing your sense of being alive. Then again, you might *want* to feel less alive because you feel overwhelmed or disappointed by life. Here is where the delicious irony comes in: The more fully present you are in the present moment, the more alive you feel, and the more alive you feel, the more you enjoy life, and the more you enjoy life, the better your life becomes.

Baba Ram Dass, nee Richard Alpert, said it most succinctly in the title of his seventies book, *Be Here Now.* It was what one of his teachers, Bhagwan Dass, would say to him repeatedly. *Be.* Exist in yourself, in the moment, in the Creator. Experience the sounds, breath, aromas, colors, meaning, energy, and feelings of the moment, without judging them either good or bad. *Here.* Not mentally or emotionally anywhere else, because there is no need. To be completely here where you are is to be everywhere with everyone in every time, because everything in the universe is connected. *Now.* Not sooner, not later, which are only illusions of the linear left brain. There is only now. The present moment is like a wormhole in space-time, a gateway to every here there is.

The richest experience is always happening right now. Be present in the present, and the present becomes a present. Inside each moment are all the gifts.

DREAM JOURNEYS

HOPES and dreams do seem to go hand in hand; at the very least you hope your dreams for the future come true. You can use the dreams you experience while you sleep to show you the lay of the land between you and your future hopes.

Dreams are journeys through the world of your inner self. They reflect your mental beliefs, emotional attitudes, and spiritual awareness. They can reveal behavior patterns, alert you to dangers, and allow emotional release.

When your conscious mind is at rest, the door is open for your supraconscious and subconscious minds to communicate with you. They speak in the language of symbolic imagery because they can convey more information more fully and accurately through symbols than through words.

Think of your supraconscious and subconscious selves as your personal tour guides on your dream journeys. Before falling asleep, tell your dream guides what you want your dreams to focus on. Perhaps you want to see how you are limiting business or relationship success. Maybe you need a physical or emotional healing, or desire information to help solve a problem. When you state what you want, then your guides can show you the most appropriate sights.

Keep a dream journey journal just as you would keep a diary on a trip. As soon as you wake up, write down the date, what you did, who and what you saw, and what you felt, even if they are just fragments. The journal will expand your understanding of your dreams. It also lets your sub- and supraconscious selves know you value what they're showing you, and they will book you on trips to view even more inspiring sights. Your journal is your ticket to first-class dreams.

WHAT DO YOU NEED?

ONE of the most powerful questions you can ask another person at any given moment, in any situation, in any language, is: What do you need? For example:

What do you need to feel better?
What do you need to accomplish your goal?
What do you need in this relationship?
What do you need to be at peace?
What do you need to feel loved?
What do you need to be fulfilled?

Asking the question immediately shows the other person that you respect and care about their well-being. The sincerity of your interest will encourage them to respond honestly, and perhaps even enable them to articulate needs they didn't know they had, which can be rewarding for you both.

Asking the question also helps prevent you from assuming that you know what another person needs, and perhaps being in error. This can save you down the road from the messes of misunderstanding.

Whenever you want to solve a problem, discovering what's needed helps to focus thinking and initiate effective action. Asking the question even when no specific problem is evident increases understanding and goodwill.

Pose the question, "What do you need?" to moody mates, harried coworkers, fretful children, and depressed friends. The results will amaze you.

When you help others to define and meet their needs, be sure to stay within your own physical, financial, and emotional means so that your needs are not strained. Helping others fulfill their needs is a good deed indeed!

EARTH SPIRIT

MANY have interpreted the Book of Revelations in the Christian bible to mean that the world is facing Armageddon. According to the Mayan calendar, a Great Cycle ends December 21, 2012, which is taken to mean that the world ends at that time. Nostradamus, in sixteenth-century France, foresaw many cataclysmic events taking place around the turn of the millennium. Native Americans have prophesied great changes in Mother Earth for the same period of time, heralded by the birth of a white buffalo, an event that has occurred.

The energy of the changes must be very powerful indeed for so many prophets and seers to have envisioned them. Some of the changes are growing pains, as the Earth is a living being and is still growing. The Earth is also changing to fulfill its purpose of supporting not only the physical evolution of human life, but the spiritual. Humankind is in the throes of opening to a new dimension of spiritual awareness and power, and the energy frequencies of the Earth are shifting to both stimulate and sustain these shifts in consciousness.

Many of the increased Earth activities are manifestations of the increase in energy taking place on the spiritual levels, but it is not necessary for those activities to be catastrophic. Be open to the probability that many of the dramatic events the prophecies refer to are spiritual, not physical. It may very well be that physical life will not end in the year 2012, but that linear, Newtonian views of the world are coming to an end, so that a new spiritual consciousness can be born. Prophecies, after all, are forecasts of probable future realities, and you and others can change the energy of those realities by raising the energy levels of all your actions so they are attuned to the spirit of the Earth.

HOME BLESSINGS

YOUR home provides shelter, one of the basic necessities of life. Having a home to live in, however humble or grand, is a boon. The fact that millions of people on the planet are homeless, makes being "homeful" a special blessing.

How often do you bless your blessing? Once a week? Once in a while? Never? To bless something is to give thanks for it, asking that it be protected and filled with happiness. Using these principles you can compose your own blessing, or adapt the following one to your personal needs:

> Thank you Creator for the shelter and comfort of my home.
> I ask your light to completely fill and surround my home,
> That it, its inhabitants, its activities, and its contents
> Are enlivened with love and kept safe in all ways.

As you say the blessing, visualize glowing white light surrounding the outside of your home. Then picture the light filling every nook and cranny of every room inside. It surrounds and fills everyone and everything in every room, and blesses all the activities. Your subconscious mind supports your mental images, creating uplifting, protective light in and around your home. Bless your home once a day to make it brighter, lighter, and safer. Wherever you stay when you travel becomes your temporary home, so bless that place, too.

Try expanding the boundaries of how you define home. In a more inclusive sense your neighborhood is also your home. So is the town or city in which you live. The state. The country. The planet Earth, too, is your home, as are the solar system, the Milky Way galaxy, and the universe. Expand the light to surround and fill your extended homes. Bless them all!

MISTAKE CHEER

Everyone who succeeds does so by making mistakes.

Mistakes can be stepping stones to success, providing you have a strategy for fixing them and learning from them. The first step is to admit to the mistake. Taking responsibility for the impact of your actions is powerful, and sets constructive energy in motion. Apologize. To the extent possible, repair any physical, financial, mental, or emotional damage your error caused. When reparations have been made, analyze where and how you went off course.

The awkward, embarrassing, perhaps even painful results of a mistake are meant to grab your attention and say, "Look at this." A mistake means that your take on a person, situation, or action missed. It could have happened because your judgment was faulty, you were not paying close enough attention, your information was incomplete, your timing was off, your assessment of the situation was inaccurate, or you misunderstood a key element. Mistakes are valuable because they show you what you need to learn or change to accomplish your objective.

The really good news is that every mistake you make shows that you are out there in life, taking action and taking risks. You are not playing it safe by doing only what you know and are secure in doing. You are trying something new, or are doing something old in a new way. Pat yourself on the back. Mistakes mean you are living life.

So seize your mistakes with gusto. Taking the risk of making a mistake is powerful. Cheer your mistakes, and they will cheer you.

LIFELINE

AWARENESS is a kind of lifeline, because it is essential for connecting you to life. The more energy that flows through your awareness, the more alive and powerful your life becomes. To increase your awareness of the patterns of your life, create a lifeline. Use several sheets of plain paper taped together end to end horizontally, or a roll of plain paper. Between the top and bottom of each paper draw a thick line from left to right so you have one long continuous horizontal line. This serves as a reference line for your life. You will write positive events above the line and negative ones below it. How far above or below the line you note an event depends on the degree of pleasure or pain you experienced.

The beginning of the horizontal line at the far left, marks the beginning of your life. Write O. If you slid into the world fairly easily, with a minimum of labor, write the word *birth* and the date near the top of the page above the far left side of the reference line. If your birth was laborious, painful, or compromised, write your birth date near the bottom of the page below the far left side of the line.

Continue to chronologically arrange important events of your life along the median line, marking your age along the line. A significant experience might be physical, mental, emotional, or spiritual: making a team, singing, graduation, jobs, love, marriage, insight, giving birth, divorce, peace, illness, or revelation.

You will continue to remember events for several days, even weeks, so allow time and room for additions. Are there more events above the line, or below? If your lifeline chart is bottom-heavy, you might want to consider making changes in the choices you make. To the right of the present date, above the lifeline, write desirable future events you want to create. Enjoy a lively lifeline.

WRITE OUT ANGER

EXPRESSING anger in a healthy way is healthy. Denying anger and bottling it up inside can lead to physical illness and mental depression. Healthy ways of releasing anger include beating up a cushion, banging pots, running fast, ripping paper, yelling into a pillow, and hitting a ball with a racquet, club, or bat.

Sometimes, however, your mind has a mind of its own, and even though you've released energy physically, your thoughts are snared in an angry loop. You constantly imagine what you really want to say to the person who hurt you, and what you want to do them. It is important to release this energy, or it will fester within you, infecting you, your relationships, and the quality of your life. Your subconscious mind, whose task it is to help create your reality based on the information it receives from your conscious mind, might even think you want all those nasty events to happen to you and create them in *your* life.

When we suppress negative thoughts we actually give them more power. Release angry mental energy by writing a no-holds barred angry letter to the person who hurt you. Be sure to write it in longhand. Let the words rip. Tell them exactly what a lowdown kind of person you think they are. Run with it. Do not censor yourself. Describe all the malevolent misfortune you wish for them. Hit them with every hostile, malicious, mean word you have in your arsenal.

Then put the letter aside for twenty-four hours. Reread the letter the next day, adding anything you forgot to say. Do *not* mail the letter. Take the pages to a place where it is safe to have a fire and burn them. Ask the Creator to heal your released anger so you are free of it and any negative connection to the person. Giving a letter a burning piece of your mind brings peace.

POWER STEERING

L**IKE** the engine in your car, power itself is neither good nor bad. It might be strong or weak, but it is how you direct your power that determines whether it has negative or positive impact. You are in the driver's seat. You can use your power to drive children to school, rob a bank, or as a status symbol. The choice is yours because you are self-determining, courtesy of the Creator. To ascertain the positive or negative impact of an action ask: Does it enhance my well-being and the well-being of others, now and in the future?

If your power car is big and fast and you use it to show off, whose well-being does it enhance? It certainly does not improve the lives of the people you try to impress, and it might intimidate someone, causing them to be afraid to use what power they have. Feeling more powerful than others may enhance your negative ego, but it does not enhance your soul, or the hearts and minds of others. The status route is closed due to not being beneficial.

If you use your power as a vehicle to rob others of their power, you commit a grave spiritual crime, because you are stealing something that was given to them with love by the Creator, as your power was given to you. The consequences are that somewhere down the road you will lose power. It will seem like a punishment, but it will be to teach you to respect your power and that of others.

The meaningfulness of your life is defined by the impact your actions have on others. If you try to take other people's power, or restrict them from using it, your life becomes meaningless. If you fuel your power with love and steer it towards helping others learn how to love and be powerful, you are enhancing the quality of life, and your own life becomes meaningful. It is your choice.

YES OR NO?

MAYBE you are trying to decide what task is best to do next. Or if this is a good time to close a deal. Or if a particular food or vitamin is good for you.

You know the correct answers, but you might not realize it because the information exists on an unconscious level. Your subconscious and supraconscious minds operate outside the confines of your conscious mind and have a bigger picture of your life than you do. They can see where you have been, where you are, and where you are going, all at the same time, but your busy conscious mind often blocks their knowledge and wisdom.

The finger-check provides a quick and easy technique for momentarily circumventing the conscious mind so the other dimensions of your mind can relay answers to you. With each hand form a circle with your thumb and middle finger. Link the two circles like a chain by opening the thumb and middle finger of one hand, then closing it through the circle formed by the other hand.

Pull your finger circles against each other. The answer *yes* can be relayed either when one circle pulls through the other, or when both circles hold firm. Decide which signal means *yes,* and *no* will be the other signal. To tell your subconscious which signal means *yes* and which means *no,* repeat the yes and no pulls a few times, saying yes or no appropriately each time to reinforce the signal.

Next, formulate a question that can only be answered either yes or no. For example, "Is now a good time for me to give Judith a call?" "Is this melon ripe enough to eat?" Pull your circles against each other to get your answer.

Does this technique work? Finger-check it!

S.A.D. TO GLAD

DURING winter when sunlight is in short supply, or in areas that are often overcast, large numbers of people have been discovered to suffer from a light deficiency syndrome known as Seasonal Affective Disorder (S.A.D). Symptoms can include depression, fatigue, anxiety, poor concentration, weight gain, and reduced sexual desire.

Studies show that such symptoms are caused by high daytime levels of the hormone melatonin. Usually melatonin is produced at night, its production regulated in the brain by the pineal gland, which is sensitive to light.

According to Jacob Liberman, author of *Light: Medicine of the Future*, the cure is to literally lighten up. Sunlight can be simulated by installing a group of six 40-watt, full-spectrum lights in your home or office. Sitting in the full-spectrum light for half an hour in the morning, eyes open, stimulates the pineal gland to produce less melatonin, and so relieves unpleasant symptoms. Make good use of the time by balancing your checkbook, reading, pursuing a creative hobby, or planning your schedule for the day.

Improvement will be felt in as few as four days, but continue to sit in full-spectrum light for as many days as natural sunlight levels are low. Instead of feeling like a bear who has been rudely awakened from winter hibernation, the light will put spring in your step.

POWER OBJECTS

EVERYTHING is energy. Solid objects are simply stored energy vibrating at a very slow rate. Whenever a powerful ceremony, or a powerful moment occurs, every object present absorbs some of the power generated by the activities of the event. The ceremony might be a birth, baptism, bat mitzvah, birthday party, wedding, healing, communion, house blessing, graduation, or funeral. The powerful moment might be a physical triumph, a psychological insight, an emotional healing, or a spiritual opening. Some places in nature are especially powerful because of the confluence of energy generated by the earth, trees, water, and sun, or because they exist at an intersection of lines of earth energy.

By taking a small object from a powerful event or place, you take the energy with you. The object can be a stone, a shell, a coin, a bead, an acorn, a button, a ribbon, a flower, sand, a feather, a piece of glass, or anything that has meaning for you. It is best to stay away from plastic because it is not as sensitive to energy as organic materials are. And avoid taking anything that defaces or harms the area.

As you collect power objects from various experiences, keep them together in a special pouch or box. To reconnect with the energy of a particular moment or place, take out the object associated with it and hold the object in your left hand to receive the energy. Breathe deeply three or four times and allow the energy stored in the object to transport you into the power of the event. Or when you feel the need to recharge or heighten your energy, hold all the objects at the same time. You can also pulverize objects and carry them with you so their collective power energizes you. Keep your power objects private and powerful.

DOMINION

IN the first chapter of the book of Genesis in the St. James version of the Christian Bible, the Creator creates the heavens and the earth, the grasses and the trees, the fish and the fowl, the beasts and creeping things. Then in verse twenty-six is written, "And God said, Let us make man in our image, after our likeness: and let them have dominion over the fish of the sea, and over the fowl of the air, and over the cattle, and over all the earth, and over every creeping thing that creepeth upon the earth."

The word used is "dominion," but somewhere along the line it went to our heads instead of our hearts, and our negative egos decided that dominion meant domination. We now try to force nature to fulfill our needs, without respecting or considering the needs of the earth. Consequently, there is no completely fresh air left anywhere on earth, it is all contaminated to some degree. Trees—especially the ones in rainforests—which are kind enough to produce the oxygen we need to live, are being cut down at the rate of several thousand acres a day. Our seas are so polluted that each year hundreds of whales and dolphins beach themselves to die. The list is tragically long. The irony is that we have sacrificed quality of the life that counts, for material quality.

The Creator has entrusted each and every one of us with the care and well-being of an entire planet, and all the life therein, every form of which has Divine consciousness. The earth nourishes us and supports our growth. Having dominion means we are responsible for nourishing and supporting the earth, now and in the future. Each week let your actions toward the earth express your respect and love. Your life depends on it.

WORD SUPPORT

COMMUNICATION is a bridge between people. When you need to solve a problem or explore an idea, the quality of communication builds either a weak bridge or a strong one, which determines the quality of the result. A weak bridge is unable to support each person's ideas, feelings, and goals, and conversational progress collapses. A strong bridge allows honest, productive exchange. Because people are connected on both conscious and unconscious levels, building a strong communication bridge involves more than just talking.

On the physical level, listen attentively and speak so the other person can understand you. If you are concerned that you have not been understood, ask the other person to paraphrase your point back to you so you can assess whether the person has grasped it, then clarify as necessary. Paraphrase the other person's points to ensure you have comprehended them accurately. Paraphrasing is especially beneficial when there is stress and conflict.

To create rapport on a more subtle level, listen to what kinds of words the other person uses—I see, I hear, I feel, or I do—and use the same words. Mirroring the other person's body language also increases harmony.

During the discussion, regularly reinforce the thought that you want the outcome to benefit both of you, and accompany it with a warm feeling of satisfaction. The other person will respond more agreeably.

Call in high-quality energy by visualizing bright white light surrounding both of you. Ask for guidance from your supraconscious self.

Taking actions on several conversational levels builds a strong bridge to support your words, allowing you to move towards understanding and resolution.

GETTING GROUNDED

WHEN you were a child you were probably reprimanded for stamping your feet. Your parents might have said it was rude, or told you to settle down. You may feel vindicated to learn that you were instinctively onto something good.

Stamping your feet centers you. When you are feeling confused or overwhelmed by events that seem to be coming at you faster than you can manage them, stamp your feet. When you are frightened by a physical or emotional threat, or feel insecure, stamp your feet. When you have been meditating, or have undergone a healing, or have had a massage, and need to focus in a hurry so you can drive your car responsibly, stamp your feet.

If you feel self-conscious about stamping your feet in front of other people, go somewhere private to do it. You can stamp your feet anywhere with good effect, but some places are better than others. The best place to do it is outdoors on the ground, preferably in bare feet. That way you connect directly with the energy of the earth, becoming literally grounded. If you are stamping your feet indoors on a floor, it helps to take off your shoes if you have time.

Be sure to stamp both feet. If you only stamp one foot it affects the energy on one side of your body, but not the other, causing an imbalance. Stamp your feet in alternation, left-right-left-right, ending the stamp with the opposite foot you started with. You will be able to feel how many times to do it. Don't stamp so hard it hurts. The impact of even a gentle stamp reverberates through your body up to your head, then travels back down, centering your attention within yourself and bringing you back to earth so you can act constructively.

MINDMARK

WHEN you travel through the physical landscape, you know where you are because you recognize landmarks. And because you know where you are, you know what turns to take to get where you are going. When you travel through your mindscape you can feel lost because it seems abstract and strange. In trying to orient yourself in mental time and space you search for something familiar, and so turn to memories of the past. The problem with this is that you might continually revisit old haunts and not explore new mental territory.

To feel more at home in your mindscape, establish a central mindmark that you can identify easily. Do this by visualizing a beautiful place that is outdoors in nature, and that makes you feel safe, strong, and sure. It can look like a physical place you have visited or be an ideal place. Your special place might be a beach, a mountaintop, a clearing in a forest, the desert, or a meadow.

Feel yourself standing in your special place. What do you see? What sounds do you hear? What aromas do you smell? What is the surface of the ground beneath your feet? Add distinctive features that uplift you, such as favorite flowers, a waterfall, or birds. This is your place of mental power. It is where you can come to clear confusion, focus, recharge your inner batteries, and connect with the power of your subconscious and supraconscious minds.

Marking a place in your mind allows you to journey wherever you want. Asking is the ticket. Ask for light to illuminate your path. Ask for a "mind guide" to appear. Ask to be shown how you are blocked. Ask for help in healing your past. Ask to see your future. Begin and end your mind journeys in your mindmark, it grounds your conscious mind and frees the rest of your mind to travel.

BETTER IS BETTER

WHEREVER you are you have three basic choices: you can leave the area the same as you found it, you can make it worse, or you can make it better. The third possibility is the best logical choice, it is also the best spiritual choice.

Whenever you make a place better, you raise the quality of energy of the whole area, helping other positive acts to occur. An area with positive energy provides a positive atmosphere for the people in it. Uplifted, they go other places and perform positive acts there. The ripple effect is just plain powerful.

Start with where you live, regardless of the size or quality of your home, or if you rent or own: repair, upgrade, or add something.

Help friends whose homes you spend time in, help them with a project they are involved in: painting, landscaping, fixing, expanding.

At work, make your space personal, pleasant, bright, clean, and efficient so it is conducive to you producing your best work.

Keep your car clean inside and out. Tune it. Change the oil.

In stores, pick up an item that has fallen on the floor and replace it on the shelf, hang clothes back on hangers, wipe the sink in rest rooms.

Outdoors, pick up other people's litter as well as your own and place it in trash receptacles. Make sure camp fires are thoroughly extinguished.

As for your home the earth, plant trees and flowers. Start a community vegetable garden. Get involved with an organization that is helping to clean up the air, a river, a lake, a beach, a park. Protect a forest. Save a whale or a wolf.

If you are unwilling or unable to improve a place, at least do no harm.

Leaving a place in better shape, leaves you in better shape, too.

COMMUNITY

Do you take pride in being independent, or are you active in a community? Any group of two or more individuals who share common interests, usually within a particular area or venue, constitutes a community. You might be a member of several communities: family, the neighborhood where you live, your workplace, or a religious center, or you might be part of a group who supports the environment, makes movies, loves dancing, studies stars, or collects coins. On the macro end of the spectrum you are a member of the state and country in which you live, the community of human beings, and the cosmic community.

Communities are powerful because of their synergy factor. When individuals work together cooperatively, they produce significantly greater results than their independent efforts would create. With synergy, $1 + 1 = 3$. The more people there are working in harmony, the more synergy they create.

In times of personal crisis—illness, injury, loss—an individual is more likely to recover if he or she is part of a community, because the other members supply support and resources. If the community as a whole is damaged by war or natural disasters, those who are unaffected, or people from a larger community pitch in to help. Individuals who are physically, mentally, emotionally, or spiritually isolated, are much less likely to survive crises.

Whatever community you belong to, become more active. This is an excellent time in the evolution of human life to learn how to combine your individual energy with that of others to contribute to the greater good. Being part of, rather than apart from, both reflects and reinforces your bond with the interconnectedness of all life in the universal community.

BEING BREATHING

WHEN was the last time you were consciously aware of your breathing? It might coincide with the last time you were really aware of being alive. Breath is life not just because we stay alive for less time without it than without water or food, but because it connects us with our core selves and with the force that created us and the universe. Breath is such a sublime gift we don't even have to consciously do anything to receive it—the air is just there, waiting for us.

A way to give thanks for your breath and life is to simply be with your breathing. Sit comfortably with your head and spine straight. Inhale. Feel your breath pass through your nose and down the back of your throat. Put aside any other thought. Feel your lungs expand with life and energy. Let all other thoughts pass by. Focus only on your breathing. Surrender to the exhalation. Become your breath. Breathe with your whole body. Breathe with the universe.

Be sure that both nasal passages are clear. The right nostril relates to your masculine energy and the left hemisphere of your brain. If it is blocked you could experience difficulty defining goals, organizing plans, and initiating action. Your left nostril relates to feminine energy and your right brain; a blockage can inhibit your ability to receive, experience emotion, and be intuitive.

Breath connects you with your feelings. In English, the letters in BREATH can be rearranged to spell B-HEART. People who are afraid of feeling certain emotions often breathe shallowly as an unconscious way of stifling their feelings. When you have pain, anger, or fear you want to release, breathe consciously.

Be a human being breathing. Be a human, being breathing.

NEW MOON SEEDING

HONORING the power of the moon is one of the most ancient rites still practiced by humankind. Farmers are aware of the moon's influence on the growth of their crops. They plant when the moon is new, using the increasing energy of the waxing moon to increase the quality and quantity of their crops

You, too, can take advantage of the moon's increasing energy to successfully grow new ideas, skills, patterns of behavior, and business projects. (Diets are the exception to this, and are best begun when the moon is waning after a full moon, so that appetite and weight decrease rather than increase.)

The Old Farmer's Almanac or an astrological calendar can tell you when a new moon is going to occur. A day or two before the new moon, gather ideas—like seeds—of the goals you want to grow. Write each seed-goal on a small piece of paper—any color or shape—in a single, positive present tense sentence, as if the goal were happening now. "I'm in charge of the Smith account." "I clearly communicate what I want." "I am loving."

To symbolize the planting of your seed-goal, on the evening of the new moon, tuck each seed-goal paper in the earth around a plant. To help the goal germinate, take appropriate physical action. You might begin piano lessons, implement a stress-reduction program, read a book on hydroponics, or initiate a business project by writing letters to those who will be involved. Combining physical and mental action also creates synergy, producing greater outcomes than either act alone.

The goals you plant when the moon is new will grow as the energy of the moon waxes. Shine the light of intention on them, and water every day with attention. New moon goals will blossom and bear fruit by the next full moon.

FULL MOON RELEASE

WITH a gravitational pull so powerful it causes all the water on the Earth to rise twice a day, the moon is a force to be respected. In addition to affecting the tides of our planetary body, the moon affects the tides of our human bodies, which are 70 percent water, including our brains.

The culmination of the full moon is naturally followed by a time of waning energy. This makes it an ideal time to let go of negative thoughts, habits, people, and circumstances because the attachment to them will decrease as the moon decreases. Here are two ways to release negativity:

1. Fill a large bowl with water and set it indoors or outdoors where it will catch the light of the full moon. Cut unlined white paper into small squares, approximately 1-inch × 1-inch. Using water soluble ink, write the name of a limitation or limiting person on a square. Place the squares of paper facedown in the bowl of water. The water dissolves the ink, releasing the limitations into the light of the full moon and freeing you of negative energy.

2. Find a quiet spot for looking at the moon, either indoors or outdoors. In your mind, picture a river of moonlight flowing from the moon to you. In front of you a boat is floating on the river, it's stern toward you. Load into the boat whatever you no longer want in your life: problems, illness, pain, fear, anger, excess weight, adversaries. If you need to, make the boat bigger to accommodate everything and everyone you want to set free. Now the moon river flows in the opposite direction, from you to the moon. Send the boat with its contrary cargo sailing up the river to the full moon. As the moon wanes the negative energy you have released into it will diminish.

NEW RELATIONSHIP VIEW

At the beginning of a new relationship, whether personal or professional, the other person will often treat you well. He or she accords you every consideration, compliments you, and might even give you gifts. To discover how deeply such niceties run, pay careful attention to how the person treats himself or herself.

The person might be a potential boss, co-worker, lover, or friend, but sooner or later they'll do unto you as they do unto themselves. Observe their behaviors and attitudes. Are they disciplined or reckless? Inflexible or tolerant? Do they take responsibility for the impact of their actions? Are they enlivened by their accomplishments? Forgiving of their mistakes? Do they seek to understand themselves? Are they generous with themselves?

You get the idea. A person who is critical of himself will eventually be critical of you. A person whose discipline borders on rigid, will not be lenient with you. If someone doesn't accept responsibility for their actions, you're the one they'll wind up blaming. On the plus side, a person who celebrates life will celebrate yours. Someone who is kind to themselves, will also be kind to you.

The maxim that you can only love another to the extent that you love yourself, still holds true. Make sure that a person loves and respects themselves before entrusting them with your heart, money, or secrets.

Being an astute observer when you are first getting to know someone creates an island of objective reality in what can be a sea of alluring illusion. You are then better equipped to decide how close you want to be with the person. Taking such precautions is also an expression of your love and respect for yourself, and enables you to continue to feel love and respect for yourself.

CHANGING IS A TRIP

Have you identified a personal quality or pattern of behavior that you are willing to change? Here's a way to help facilitate the change process. It's a trip!

Plan an excursion somewhere new, an hour or more away by car, bus, plane, or train. Walking or traveling on horseback doesn't take you far enough away to create the necessary impact. It will heighten the process if your destination is a beautiful place in nature, but a pretty spot in a city will also work.

Before leaving, write down what it is you want to change. On another piece of paper write a description of how you will look, feel, and behave differently when you are different. How will your interactions with others be different? What will you be able to create in your life? Pack both papers.

Leave home, taking your frailties with you. Use the travel time to think about how your limitation has limited you. Understand the fear and pain that created the condition to begin with. Forgive yourself. Be grateful for the aspects of yourself you like and which further you, and which you want to keep.

When you arrive at your destination, seek out a naturally beautiful area. Sometimes a cemetery is an appropriate spot for such a change. Read the paper on which you wrote your definition of what you want to change. Write "RELEASED" across it in big block letters. Tear the paper into tiny pieces and release them into water, fire, the wind, or bury them in the earth.

Read the paper describing your new self. In this new place, where you are not bound by routines and other people's expectations, do something as your new self, that your old self wouldn't have done. Celebrate. On the return trip, think about how the change you have made will improve and expand your life.

MALE-FEMALE

REGARDLESS of what gender your body is, you have both masculine and feminine qualities. Carl Jung referred to the masculine self as the *animus*, and the feminine self as the *anima*. Chinese philosophers call female energy *yin*, and male energy *yang*. In romance languages such as Spanish and French, every noun is either masculine or feminine according to its function and shape.

Some of the key characteristics of masculine energy include: initiating, positive polarity, light, cold, straight line, conscious, and reason. Key feminine characteristics include: receiving, negative polarity, darkness, heat, circle, unconscious, and emotion. The masculine also relates to the right side, and the feminine to the left side. That's why at weddings friends of the groom sit on the right side, and friends of the bride sit on the left.

Because everything is connected, knowledge of these qualities is especially helpful when you want to understand the underlying forces behind physical illness or injury. If the right side of your body is affected, masculine principles are active. If the left side is affected, feminine principles are involved. For example, if your right hand is disabled, it could be the result of not initiating reaching out. If your left knee hurts, you might be feeling hurt because you have not received the support you need to help you cope with the impact of an event.

To charge and balance your energy each day, engage in both masculine and feminine activities. Give and receive, talk and listen, be rational and intuitive, active and peaceful, be warm, be cool. The purpose of opposites is not to create conflict, but to create movement of energy so you can progress into greater harmony with yourself, others, the earth, and the Creator.

DESIRE DETACHMENT

DESIRE is essential to success. If you don't desire to buy a new car, play a sport well, increase understanding in a relationship, or connect with your higher self, you probably won't. Desire sets energy in motion and gets the attention of both your subconscious and supraconscious minds, thereby enlisting their aid.

Some people try to avoid having desires because they believe that desire lies at the root of suffering. That can be true, but usually only if you remain attached to the act of desiring, or to the outcome of your desire. It is these attachments that create frustration and distress, not the desire itself.

Without desire life would be pretty lifeless. Desires abound, consciously and unconsciously. Your body desires food and air. Your mind desires ideas and stimuli. You desire a home to shelter you, love to uplift you. Your higher self desires that you consciously connect with the Creator.

Desiring something is like turning the ignition key in your car. Once you have turned it and the engine is running, if you keep turning it you damage the engine. So, yes, with your whole heart and a bright mind desire your goals, be they lofty or mundane, then let go of the desire and get on with driving your life.

Once desire has set you in motion, do not be attached to how the objective of your desire manifests. You used free will to choose your destination, but as you are driving there, let go of what you expect to happen when you arrive, with whom, and how. Give it to the Creator to create whatever is for your greatest good, trusting that the Creator has a broader picture of the purpose of your life than your conscious mind. This frees you to focus on your driving, and allows you to arrive at your objective ready for life and open to learning and love.

CONFESSION

CONFESSION is good for the soul. Centuries ago the Catholics thought it was so powerful they created a ritual to help people unburden themselves of wrongdoing. Fortunately you do not have to be Catholic to benefit.

Just about everyone has done something, somewhere, sometime, of which they are ashamed. Keeping the shameful act hidden inside you is like planting a seed of dark negative energy. The kernel is the conflict between what you believe is proper behavior and the act you committed that doesn't measure up. You might also have lied to protect your secret, or committed other acts to cover it up, increasing the size and force of the dark seed.

Even if you shut your mind to it, the seed continues to grow within you. The negativity feeds on your positive energy, weakening you, and permeates your body, your thoughts, and your feelings. Eventually your entire system becomes clogged, and you are increasingly separated from sources of love.

Confessing your shameful deed is equivalent to reaching inside and pulling it out by its roots. Confess first to yourself. Say aloud, in private, "I did. . . ." Or write it down. Even doing just this much strengthens you because you are acknowledging truth. You can then confess to an officiating member of your religion, or go right to the source and confess to the Creator. Tell the Creator how you feel about having done the deed. Express your remorse. Ask for forgiveness. Depending on the degree of sincerity of your regret, you may have the sensation of being flooded with love, feel a heaviness being lifted from you, or feel lighter, stronger, freer, and more peaceful.

PERMISSION TO HELP

THERE are so many people who need help, and so many ways to extend help to them. Sometimes a kind word is enough, but often a more substantial action is called for. You might want to drive someone where they need to go, cook for them, assist them with a task, help take care of their children, offer an observation or insight about their behavior, give or loan money, buy food, donate clothes, teach them how to do something, or help heal them in some way.

No matter how honorable and kind-hearted your intentions, do not assume that the person wants to be helped simply because you are willing and able to offer assistance. Whether the person is a family member, friend, co-worker, neighbor, or stranger, first ask them if they want help. This allows them to focus on themselves and their situation, and gives them the power of deciding whether they want help. If they don't, respect their decision.

If they do, then ask if it is all right for you to help them. Soliciting their permission shows respect, allowing them to have dignity. It also makes them more receptive to receiving help, which makes it easier for you to give it, because energy follows the path of least resistance.

Everyone has the free will to decide what they want to do and what they don't want to do. It is a measure of the respect the Creator has for us that It gave us the powerful gift of free will, and it furthers us to demonstrate the same respect for each other and for each other's free will. Your high self and your angels do. They lovingly wait until you ask them for help before giving it. Native American medicine people do not teach or heal without first being asked. When it comes to helping, let others exercise their free will before you exercise yours.

EYE TO EYE

THE eyes are so closely connected to the brain that looking into someone's eyes is almost like looking directly into their mind. Combine that with French philosopher Descartes' belief that the seat of the soul is the pineal gland located in the heart of the brain, and it is easy to understand why people refer to the eyes as being the windows of the soul.

When you are talking with someone, where do you look most of the time? At their feet, your fingernails, their mouths, or at the air to the left of their souls? Does the conversation flow smoothly or does it seem to stop and start with awkward pauses. How much of what the other person says do you remember? How much do you care about the other person?

If you are not looking the person in the eye, the conversation is probably as scattered as your focus, and it is doubtful that you remember much of what has been said. Lack of eye contact conveys to the person that you care very little about them and what they have to say. If you are uncomfortable with the person, or nervous about the conversation, not looking at them emphasizes that.

If these are not the messages you want to communicate, the quick and easy solution is to look right into the person's eyes. You will immediately sense a shift in energy, because you are now connected brain to brain. As you focus on the person, you will be able to focus more clearly on what they are saying and what you are saying, and so will they. Your more focused energy raises the energy level for both of you, helping to lift and smooth the flow of conversation. You will also see behind the words to the truth of who they are, and they are empowered to do the same. In some cultures it is considered rude to look a person in the eye because making eye contact is indeed making "I" contact.

POSITIVE THOUGHT POWER

You've probably heard it a thousand times—think positive! The reason you've heard it so often is because positive thoughts are indeed powerful. It is a scientific fact that thinking stimulates electrical energy, and that different kinds of thoughts produce different wavelengths of energy such as alpha or theta waves. The electric activity produced by the brain generates an electromagnetic field of energy. What isn't often discussed is that this electric field will attract to you people and situations of like energy.

The bad news is that if you have those lowdown what's-the-use negativity blues, you are apt to attract more of the same. The good news is that you can break the downward spiral of negative thinking by thinking positive thoughts. Think a single positive thought, and then another. Remember a happy time, or an anticipated future event. Think about someone you care about, or who cares about you. Think a positive thought about yourself. No matter how mundane the positive thought—even, "I liked the cereal I ate this morning"—it will have a higher vibration of energy than a negative thought. Of course, the more emotionally positive the thought, the better.

You can also do something physically positive to spark positive thoughts. Go somewhere that is so beautiful you cannot help but notice, no matter how bleak your mood. Delve into something that fascinates you. Go to a museum or a library. See a funny movie. Help someone.

The higher energy level of positive thoughts attracts higher quality people, experiences, and opportunities to you. It also increases your feeling of well-being, and travels outward to uplift those around you and even the planet.

WHAT DO I NEED?

I F "What do you need?" is one of the most powerful questions you can ask another person, asking, "What do *I* need?" is one of the most powerful questions you can ask yourself. For example:

What do I need to feel better?
What do I need to be closer to this person?
What do I need to work more efficiently?
What do I need to complete this task?
What do I need to be healthy?
What do I need to be happy in this relationship?
What do I need to be at peace?
What do I need to feel loved?
What do I need to be fulfilled?

Asking yourself what you need when you feel stuck, stymied, or steamrolled, immediately shifts your attention within you, where the truth and solutions lie. Once you define your needs, the best actions to take to meet them become clearer. The intention here is not to be selfish or self-absorbed, but to solve the problem in a way that is positive for you and others. Taking the active step of asking, "What do I need?" will give you a greater sense of strength and calm in what may be a stressful or even chaotic situation.

If you are not used to paying attention to your needs, you might have to repeat the question a few times before the answers within you begin to surface. Sometimes just being able to articulate needs you might not have known you had can be a powerful breakthrough.

Be sure to keep the actions you decide to take, within your emotional, physical, and financial boundaries so you don't create more stress. Helping yourself fulfill your needs is a great deed indeed!

BREAKING ROUTINES

Maybe you read the title of this chapter and thought you were having enough trouble establishing routines, let alone breaking them. But people tend to be creatures of habit, and there are bound to be things you do the same way every day. The way you get dressed, peel a banana, the route you take to work, school, or the store, the foods you eat, phrases you say, what you do on Sundays, and what you wear to bed at night, are probably fairly habitual.

Habits and routines are easy, because you can do them without having to think too much about them. This is a good news/bad news situation. When you are busy, low-maintenance activities feel less stressful. The bad news is that your negative self lures you into routines to keep you from being too alive.

Your negative self is the ornery, destructive part of you whose goal is to keep you disempowered. It draws people and situations into your life to squash your power. It siphons power away from your true heart and spirit and fills itself. It dulls you so you are less inclined to take constructive action.

The good news about the bad news is that you are inherently stronger than your negative self. The more aware, alive, and active you are, the stronger you become. Embrace life more fully by breaking your routines, weakening the negative ego's hold on you. Put on your clothes in a different order. Peel the banana differently. Vary the routes you take. Staying within your dietary guidelines, try new foods or combinations. Upgrade your vocabulary. Do something completely new on Sunday, or Wednesday. Wear new nightwear.

Take the power of discovery, fun, and aliveness these simple changes spark, and fill your heart and spirit. Small positive steps lead to big triumphs.

DIRECT REQUESTS

WHAT do you do when you want something? Maybe you want someone to do something for you, or you need acknowledgment, or maybe you just want a hug or a glass of water. Do you manipulate someone into doing what you want by offering a reward, or by making them feel guilty or afraid? Or do you decide to do without what you want, rather than risk being rebuffed or disappointed?

Trying to meet your needs through manipulation causes resentment and powerlessness all the way around because it is not a constructive act, and everyone knows it on some level. It might improve your well-being in the short run, but not in the long run, and it does not improve anyone else's well-being. In effect, manipulative actions say: "I don't think enough of myself to expect to get what I want, so you probably don't think enough of me to give it to me without extra incentives or pressure."

Is this the attitude of a powerful person? Not at all. The person who is confident of themselves and their power to create good, asks for what they want directly. They know if they do not receive what they ask for they have the power to initiate other constructive action to accomplish their goal.

If you need help from a relative, friend, neighbor, co-worker, angel, or the Creator, ask clearly and directly. "Could you please. . . . ?" "May I please have . . . ?" Being clear and direct about what you want reinforces your respect for yourself and others, and their respect for themselves and you. Nobody likes being manipulated. Manipulating someone makes them and you feel tight and gray, and has a heavy feeling. Making a direct request requires less energy, and feels light and bright. It enlivens the power needed to satisfy your needs.

SURVIVING CHANGE

THE earth is always changing, but many ancient and modern prophecies point to the years surrounding the millennium as a time when significant changes are to occur. One of the areas of concern regarding these changes is how best to handle them. Who is to survive and how?

You may think you will survive, where others will not, because you are smarter, stronger, more special, or more enlightened. Thinking that you are more deserving of life than even one other person is an attitude generated by your lower negative ego, not by your loving higher self. Your negative ego tries to keep you powerless by keeping you separate. It tricks you into thinking you are better than others, which separates you from them, which separates you from life, which separates you from the Creator of life. Separation opposes the connectedness of all life, and so is not life supporting. Your negative ego also neglects to point out that among those whom you think of as poor shlubs, who are not smart-strong-special-enlightened enough to survive an Armageddon, are people whom you care about. Is that the reality you want to help create?

Earth changes are not designed to provide an opportunity for you to prove your superiority, or to punish you or anyone else, but so that you and the earth can grow and more fully express Divine Love. To that end and beginning, the Creator will help you be exactly where you need to be, when you need to be there, to experience that which is for your highest good. However, if you choose separation and suffering, the Creator may allow you that experience, out of respect for your free will. The safest place of all, is to be living in your heart, in loving harmony with all life. Invite guidance. Trust it when it comes.

LETTER TO THE FUTURE

THE universe is energy vibrating at different frequencies. Like a mini-universe you, too, are energy. Among the clusters of energy in your system is your future self. Your logical left brain cannot see the future because its perspective of time is fragmented, but your right brain sees your future self now.

Energy cannot be created or destroyed, but you can alter future energy through physical, mental, emotional, and spiritual actions. To act on all four levels, and cross the bridge between the verbal left brain and the intuitive right brain, write a letter to your future self. Write the letter in longhand to make the hand-brain connection. Then choose which future self you want to write to: the one who exists a year from now, or five years, ten years, or more. Put today's date in the upper left hand corner, and the future date in the upper right. The salutation could be, "Dear Future (your first name)."

You are writing to your most intimate friend, who knows you better than anyone, so write honestly from your heart. Do you hope your future self is happy, healthy, and wealthy? Write that. Do you hope your future self is loved and loving? Truly powerful? Write that. Write specifics. "I hope you are enjoying the house you built, the dream job, or the child you had." The clarity and strength of your present thoughts about the future help the energy of your future self to be clear and strong. Ask your future self for assistance in creating a successful future. Save the letter and reread it three times a year, and especially on the date you've written in the upper right hand corner. Do the letter and the reality match?

Your future friend is only a heartbeat and a thought away. Be open to your future self's reply in the form of sudden insights, good fortune, and illuminating dreams.

PICTURE OF SUCCESS

Your subconscious, the workhorse of your mental system, helps your mental images to manifest in the physical world. Because it speaks fluent "Imagerese," the more dynamic and informative your mental image of success is, the more powerful and complete your success will be when it appears.

Your subconscious sees the past, present, and future all at the same time, whereas the logical left brain sees time in sequential segments. To your subconscious, the future is happening now, so when it receives a clear mental picture of your goal, it thinks it is real and present. It also operates on the directive that physical and mental images of the same thing must be in harmony with each other. When it does not receive an image from the physical world that corresponds with the mental image, it sets about making your physical world match your mental world.

To enliven your mental image of success, create a collage of pictures that depict various aspects of your goal. You can cut the pictures out of magazines. If, for example your goal is to have a new home, cut out pictures of the style of home you like, exterior and interior, front and back. Also cut out pictures of people doing things at home you would enjoy doing. Include a picture of a dinner party, or someone working in a home office. The more colorful the pictures are, the better. Paste a photo of yourself over one of the people in the pictures, and paste the picture in the center of a large sheet of construction paper. Then glue the other pictures around the center one, as if they were petals of a flower. Because your subconscious processes information in clusters, this arrangement is more effective than a linear sequence. Hang the success flower on a wall. Your subconscious gets the picture, matches the physical to it, and success blooms.

PROBLEM REPAIR

IF you saw a hole in the floor of your living room, what would you do? Fix it immediately? Walk around it? Hide it under a rug? Pretend it wasn't there?

The existence of a problem, or of a difficult emotion such as anger or pain, is like having a hole in a room of your life. The hole might start out being fairly small, making it all too easy to avoid. You step over it or walk around the edges of it. You throw other activities over it—work, exercise, food, alcohol, drugs—to hide it from yourself and others. You might even deny it's there.

Days, weeks, even months go by. The problem hole grows larger because you haven't attended to it. It could cause areas around it to deteriorate. It could even begin to weaken the very foundation of your being.

One day you're walking through your life and you forget the hole problem is there. You step in the hole and fall and hurt yourself. The hole could also trip and injure someone close to you. What do you do? Curse the hole? Avoid going into that room of your life? Move out of the house?

None of these responses solves the problem. The most constructive solution is to acknowledge that the problem or emotion exists, and set about fixing it. What physical, mental, emotional, and spiritual tools and materials do you need? Write them down. Which ones do you have on hand? If you need help, call someone who is equipped to make such repairs such as a doctor, therapist, or member of the clergy.

The best solution is to take action when you first notice the problem or emotion. A small hole is considerably easier to fix than a large one. By paying attention immediately, you avoid paying a much dearer price later on.

DREAM—TAKE TWO

WHAT do you do when you have a dream you do not want to have come true? Maybe you dreamed that you lost someone or something, were hurt, received bad news, a relationship was fraught with conflict or came to an end, or you were prevented from doing something you were trying to accomplish.

Such disquieting dreams can be warnings from your subconscious. They tell your conscious mind what your thoughts and fears are creating on the subconscious level that could manifest in your physical reality.

If you have the power to create the scenario in the first place, it means you also have the power to recreate it differently. Think of your dream as a movie, with you as the director. Instead of watching the dailies, you have just seen the nightlies, and they are unacceptable. Imagine that you take the dream into an editing room and cut the sequences you don't like out of the film. You then film new sequences, with positive, uplifting, successful action and dialogue. You eliminate obstacles and provide characters with everything they need to fulfill their goals. Direct your dream movie exactly the way you want it to be, then splice the new sequences into the original dream. Hand the new version to the projectionist, who is your subconscious, and screen the dream again. You applaud the second take, delighted with the happy ending.

Consciously going back into a subconscious dream and replacing unfortunate dream sequences with beneficial ones, will influence what takes place in your waking reality. By redirecting dream scenes, you also can see your life as the conscious dream it is. This perspective empowers you to rescript and redirect the scenes in the waking dream of your life.

HEARTLAND

IMAGINE that love is tangible and has a specific location, how far away from love do you live? Next door? Down the block? Across town? In another state? In another country? On another planet? How often do you visit? Or do you live in the same house with love? In the same room?

How close or far away you are depends on how comfortable or uncomfortable with love you are. If you grew up feeling loved, and saw love in action among the people around you, then you feel safe with love. If you grew up knowing mostly hate, anger, rejection, betrayal, fear, or pain, then love is going to make you uneasy, and you will stay as far away from it as you can.

Living without love is like living on the planet Pluto; you exist but you are too far away from the light and warmth of the sun to flourish. Or you might be living in the same country as love, but in a state of depression. Fortunately, no matter how far removed from love you have become, the love in your soul never dies, and it knows the way home. Let it light your way. Let it unlock the door to loving actions. Let it lead you to loving people. Let it feed you. Let it warm you.

Begin the journey by deciding you want to return to the heartland. Obtain a ticket by asking for help from earth angels and heavenly ones. Love is within you, so all you need to pack is truth. Travel light by giving your old fears and pains to the Light to be healed. As you move closer to the sun, its light burns away the dross of fear, ego, and illusion that separate you from love.

Love gives your life meaning. It is vital to your evolution. Love inspires your actions. It teaches you and enlightens. It connects you with your spirit and with the Creator. Live deeply in the heart of love.

MIRROR WRITING

MIRROR writing is writing words backwards so they can be read when held up to a mirror. It is often dismissed as simply a parlor trick, or as the peculiar providence of a few gifted individuals. It's a shame that an activity that yields so many benefits has been so neglected. Mirror writing encourages you to take risks, exercises your brain, may help balance left and right brain activity, increases mental clarity, sparks creativity, and enhances self-esteem.

More people can mirror write than think they can—it's just a matter of trying. If you can't, only you will know. If you can, think of what you'll gain.

It helps to sit at a desk or table when mirror writing. Use an 8½-inch × 11-inch pad of either unlined paper or graph paper, positioned horizontally. Hold a pen in each hand. It will be easier to see what you've written if each pen writes in a different colored ink. Suspend the belief that you can't write backwards.

Begin by writing the most familiar words; your first and last names. Starting in the middle of the page, write your name with each hand *at the same time*. This means your right hand is writing towards the right as your left hand is writing towards the left. You'll find that your left hand naturally tracks with what the right hand is writing, even though it's writing backwards. For left-handed people this can be a bit tricky because they'll be writing forward with their right hand instead of their left. If it seems easier, print your name first, then try writing it in script. If your backward writing looks the way it did when you were eight, it's because that hand-brain connection hasn't developed—but it can!

After several tries, check what you've written by holding the paper up to a mirror. You'll be pleasantly surprised and mentally energized.

SHAKING HANDS

NEXT to your brain, your hands are the most versatile parts of your body. To mention a few of their many talents: they touch, feel, write, grasp, hold, lift, push, pull, caress, heal, draw, sculpt, play piano, and wave hello and good-bye. Clearly, your hands are directly and powerfully connected to your brain. If your brain also serves to connect you with the nonphysical world, and your feet connect you with the earth, then your hands are for connecting with others. Be sure to reach out and touch someone every day. Shake hands with someone, pat a child, caress a loved one, stroke a cat. A touch is truly worth a thousand words.

Your hands are also positive and negative battery terminals for the energy stored in the molecules of your body. The left hand is the negative terminal and the right is the positive. This also corresponds to the yin-yang approach, which says that the left side of your body is the feminine side and the right side is the masculine, except for your brain where it is switched. This means that when you touch someone you receive their energy with your left hand, and give them energy with your right. That's why in many cultures people shake right hands, strengthening the greeting by giving each other energy, and why the Buddha has his right hand raised and facing out, and his left hand is down and receptive.

When you touch someone, whether in greeting, affection, or healing, there is a definite exchange of energy. If you feel you have received negative or discordant energy, you can slough it off by shaking your hands as if trying to shake water off them. Shaking your hands all around is also good for releasing tension and getting energy circulating in them. Clenched hands inhibit the free flow of energy, so keep them open. Shake energy into your hands and the hands of others.

LIGHTING THE DARKNESS

IF you are a human being you will probably undergo at least a few periods of emotional darkness. Such times do not mean you are a failure or a hapless person, they mean that you are a feeling, evolving being. Even enlightened beings have braved dark nights of the soul. The actions you take during a bleak time determine whether the experience weakens you or strengthens you.

Honoring your emotions by identifying them and allowing yourself to feel them is beneficial, because depression is sometimes caused by anger and hurt you have not allowed yourself to express. When the energy of the pain and outrage have nowhere to go, they continually loop back on you. Just remember, when releasing emotional energy, do so in ways that do not harm yourself, others, or property: cry, scream, beat up your sofa, or hit a ball.

There may be interludes, however, when the darkness is so dense and overwhelming that you feel incapable of taking physical or emotional action. To prevent yourself from being sucked into a downward spiral, take mental action. Light a single positive thought. It does not have to be a big positive thought to work. Think about any event in your life that has made you the least bit happy. Thinking one positive thought is like lighting the proverbial candle in the darkness. That one bright thought casts back the darkness, even if just a little.

Then think another positive thought. The light of that one joins with the light of the first, creating a synergy of light brighter than either thought by itself. The light of two bright thoughts can be a beacon that summons angels to your side. Ask them, the Creator, and your high self for the help you need.

PERSONAL CYCLES

Y ou are part of creation and nature. Like the sun, you have periods when you shine more brightly and less brightly. Like the moon, there are times when your energy waxes and wanes. Like the tides, your emotions ebb and flow.

Determining when your physical, mental, and emotional energies are at their zenith, and when they are at their nadir, can help you plan your activities more effectively. For example, you would want to schedule meetings at a time of day when your physical and mental energies tend to be at a peak.

Track the ups and downs of your energy for a full month. Use a notebook with plenty of pages, and label it "Personal Cycles." Use it only for that purpose. Record how you feel at different times of the day and night, organizing the information however is easiest for you. You can simply put the day's date at the top of the page and write down how you feel throughout your waking hours, noting the time of each entry. Be sure to note your mental and emotional experiences as well as your physical. For easy reference, you might use red ink for physical, blue for mental, and green for emotional. The descriptions do not need to be elaborate, phrases will do. Or devise a system of symbols, perhaps a scale of one to five, with one being low energy and five being high. As there are other factors that influence energy besides the time of day, such as foods consumed and stressful situations, note those as well.

At the end of the month, reread your journal. Divide a new page into sections for morning, noon, afternoon, evening, and night. In the appropriate section, mark a plus for every high energy event, and a minus for every low. You will be able to see at a glance the pattern of your personal energy cycles.

WITHOUT BLAME

WHEN something goes awry between you and someone else, it can seem so easy to make it the other person's fault. Even when something goes wrong and no one else is involved, you might try to put the blame on someone or something else such as the weather, a malfunctioning computer, traffic, or illness.

If you are resistant to accepting responsibility, part of the reason might be because you view it as a burden. *Webster's Dictionary* even lists the word "burden" as a synonym for responsible. *Webster's* also gives as one of the definitions for responsible: "able to answer for one's conduct and obligations."

In terms of personal power, the definition is more accurate than the synonym. Being willing and able to answer for one's actions is a boon, not a burden. When you make someone or something else wrong, so you don't have to be, you give away your power to act. That leaves you holding the victim bag, because by making others responsible for the wrong, you give them the power to make it right. If they choose not to, you are a duck out of luck.

Instead of putting yourself at the mercy of someone or something else, take your power back by taking full responsibility for what has happened. It helps to remember that on some level you created the problem. Physical reality is really energy moving at slow rates of speed, and that energy is influenced by the energy of your thoughts, beliefs, emotions, and needs. If you were able to mentally create the predicament, you can also create the solution.

Delete the whole concept of blame from your vocabulary. Taking responsibility for your actions does not burden you, it frees and empowers you.

MIRACLES

ALBERT Einstein said, "There are two ways to live your life. One is as though nothing is a miracle. The other is as if everything is."

Which way do you live? Do you wake up dreading the day ahead, or glad for the miracles of light and life? All life, including yours, is a miracle. The plant growing on your windowsill, the tree on the street, are miracles. Sunrises and moonrises are miracles. Love is a miraculous feeling. Water flowing from your faucet or down your cheeks is a miracle. Ideas. Sunlight. Smiles. Sighs. A friendly touch. Lions and spiders. A song. Fire. Languages. Breath. Death. The opportunities for experiencing miracles are infinite, it's a matter of attitude.

Miraculous events that defy rational explanations—which is exactly their point—are in a whole other class. There are documented miracles where people are saved from fatal falls by unseen forces, tumors are healed spontaneously, shipwrecked sailors are saved by dolphins, and lost children are kept warm by a dog. Such dramatic events take place outside the logical, linear thinking of the left brain. If you insist that reality adhere strictly to reason, to be parsed and analyzed, you obstruct the manifestation of miracles.

The creative, emotional, spontaneous right-brain is your connection to miracles. Let go of the limiting, imprisoning left-brain belief that miracles are impossible, and move over to the belief that everything is possible. It's a move up. Then, with all your heart, ask for miracles to occur. Asking for help with sincere, strong intention gives the angelic forces, the messengers of the Creator, permission to perform the miracles that are for your highest good.

Open the doors of your beliefs to miracles, extend heartfelt invitations, and you will welcome miracles into your life.

SYMBOL POWER

UNIVERSAL symbols—those shared by all people—are powerful because they are timeless and succinct. They cross all language barriers, speaking directly to the unconscious mind without becoming tangled in the web of words spun by the conscious mind. Carl Jung believed symbols to be the true spiritual language.

Create a personal symbol to reinforce who you want to become, or a goal you want to achieve. Some of the basic symbolic shapes to draw from are the circle, straight line, semi-circle, cross, triangle, diamond, star, and arrow.

Religious, scientific, and astrological symbols, as well as numbers, are derived from combinations of the two essential shapes, the circle and the straight line. The circle represents the beginning and the end, the all, the soul, completion, eternity. A line represents self and consciousness. A vertical line is decisive action and masculine. A horizontal line is the earth, passive, feminine. A triangle pointed up is evolution. A five-pointed star is a human, a six-pointed star is fire and water combined. A cross is spirit into and out of matter, higher and lower selves.

Experiment. Draw different combinations of the above symbols, choosing two to four shapes that you feel embody qualities pertinent to you or your quest. It's best not to use too many, or to make the configuration too complicated, because it can be difficult to process effectively when you look at it.

When you have created a symbol that feels as if it speaks to you and empowers you, draw it on sheets of paper (white or colored) or index cards. Post them in various places around your home and office. The more often you see your personal symbol throughout the day, the more it will become part of you and awaken the essence of its power in you.

RICH RELATIONS

W HEN you are sick it is not your money, house, car, or status that holds your hand and makes you soup. It is people who care for you. Such human beings are gems and constitute a large percentage of your true wealth. Polish up your relationships and make them shine by letting people you love know that you love them. Say the words, "I love you." Don't wait to do it, because you cannot be certain that tomorrow will bring another opportunity.

Also, when someone does something that makes you feel good, let them know. Why keep it a secret? Acknowledging that another person's actions had a positive effect on you does not give them more power and diminish yours, as some people mistakenly believe. It actually increases power all the way around in a handsome, synergistic sort of way. You were, in fact, being powerful to begin with by creating the opportunity to receive something you needed or wanted. The other person was being powerful by doing the thing that made you feel good. Saying thank you is a positive action that is itself powerful and makes you feel good. Expressing your appreciation makes the other person feel good, reinforcing their enjoyment of acting powerfully and inspiring them to act positively again, on your behalf or someone else's.

All these actions combined create more goodwill and powerful energy than any one action by itself. That's synergy. Make it a point to let others know the positive ways they make a difference in your life.

The more generously you appreciate other people, the more the value of your own life appreciates, paying rich relationship dividends.

TAKE IT TO HEART

SOMEONE says, "That suit looks great on you." What do you say? "Thank you," or, "I'm about to donate it to the thrift store." Someone tells you how much he or she appreciates your efforts. What do you say? "I was glad to do it," or, "I should have done more."

If you have trouble accepting compliments, you are not alone. You are among millions of people who believe that accepting praise is egotistical, that your head will swell. Yet belittling a compliment is akin to telling the person who gave it that they have lousy judgment. It's as if someone hands you a gift and you tell them they have poor taste and hand the gift back, belittling them and their gesture, all because you wanted to avoid an inflated ego.

Better ways of handling compliments exist. Your best bet, just from the perspective of being polite, is to simply say, "Thank you," and smile. There are deeper levels of acceptance operating as well. Compliments and positive feedback are food for the spirit. To reject them is to deny yourself nourishment.

You know that the most practical way to eat food is to put it in your mouth. The most effective way to eat a compliment is to put it in your heart. Taste the flavor of it, swallow it, and digest it. Your heart will feel pleasantly full.

But how do you know a compliment has gone to your heart and not to your negative ego? Easy. If you catch yourself thinking you are better than others, your negative ego has taken the compliment. Your negative ego defines itself by comparing itself to others, finding itself either "less than" or "more than." "Than" is the red flag word to listen for. Your true heart is secure within itself and has no need or inclination to compare itself. Feel free to take compliments to heart, it is satisfying and filling.

CHILD TIME

Time is a matter of perspective. Your analytical left brain needs to process time logically, breaking time down into past, present, and future segments which follow each other in a line. Your right brain is not similarly constrained. It sees time as circular, with events as clusters or patterns of energy that exist at the same time. To view an event with your right brain, you simply shift your attention.

An example is reading a book. You are now focusing your attention on the event of this particular page, which is a pattern of energies, but the entire book still exists. Your left brain sees only this page, but your right brain sees the whole book, beginning, middle, and end.

Similarly, your attention is focused on who you are now, but your entire self—past, present, and future—exists at the same time. This means that your child self is alive and active. The quality of energy of your child self can influence the energy of your present self. If your child self is happy, playful, and creative, you can bring those qualities into your present experiences. If your child self is sad and frightened, you could be bringing that energy into your life.

An easy way to pass through the door of your right brain into its time room, is to create a mental image of yourself as a child. See what you are wearing, how your hair is cut, and the expression on your face. Say, "Hi." You, of course, are your child-self's future self, but it is best to introduce yourself as a friend.

Ask your child self how they are feeling. Is your child-self sad or glad? Does your child-self need a hug? Ask what he or she needs and wants and give it to your child-self with no strings attached. Whatever ways you bring comfort, healing, and joy to your child-self, you do the same for your present and future selves, all in good time.

SAY IT SAFE

During the course of a day you say hundreds, maybe thousands of sentences. What percentage of those statements are positive? One hundred percent? Ninety percent? Fifty percent? Twenty-five percent? Ten percent?

What percentage of your life is positive? It is probably about the same as your percentage of positive statements. The reason for this is that your subconscious mind hears and records every sentence you say, and helps them manifest physically, because that is what it is programmed to do. It does not evaluate their positive or negative worth—that's the job of your conscious mind—it just manifests them. This is what makes negative sentences so dangerous.

The computer expression, "Garbage in, garbage out" really applies here. If you verbally download negative data into your subconscious, that is what will come out in your life. Also keep in mind that your subconscious does not compute negative sentence structure, and it acts only on key words. If your nose starts feeling stuffy you might say, "I sure hope I don't get sick!" Your subconscious records, "I hope I get sick!" and does its job by helping you to be sick. Presto, you come down with a terrible cold. The same effect holds true for, "I bet my boss is going to reject my proposal." "With my luck it will rain on my party." Or if you repeatedly say, "I am sick and tired of: waiting, working late, being treated badly," you will spend most of your time being sick, tired, and waiting, working late, and being treated badly.

Instead, say it safe: "I am healthy." "My boss loves my proposal." "It is sunny during my party." "I am healthy, energetic, and in charge of my life." Simply by deleting negative sentences and downloading positive ones, you can begin today to improve the quality of your life. What you say is what you get!

GOAL POEM

Regardless of whether you know iambic pentameter, writing a poem focuses your thoughts, helps reveal your feelings, expands creativity, gets the attention of your subconscious, and raises your energy level at least a couple of octaves. When the subject of your poem is a goal you want to achieve, all those benefits are bestowed upon your goal.

Pick one goal from what is probably a long mental list—you can always write poems about other goals down the road. Be sure to choose the goal you truly want—the one most connected to your heart—not the one you think you should want, or that someone else wants you to achieve. The goal might have to do with business, income, a personal relationship, physical health, mental health, love, personal growth, or spiritual awareness.

Begin by simply jotting down phrases that describe your goal, how you will feel about attaining your goal, and how this success will affect your circumstances and empower you. Once you have the basics down on paper, play with the phrases, arranging them in poem form. The poem can be in free verse, or if rhyming comes easily to you, rhyme away.

The poem does not have to be perfect or good, just clear and sincere. Avoid making the poem long and complicated, because that gives your subconscious the message that you want the process of achieving your success to be long and complicated. Keep the poem short, easy, and from your heart.

Say your poem aloud every day until you achieve your goal. If you like to sing, singing your goal poem will add even more oomph. Say it or sing it at the beginning of your day and at the end. Your success is sure to be poetic.

SERVICE WITH A SMILE

YOUR life is busy, full, and complicated, and it requires huge doses of energy and attention. In terms of the bigger picture, it is one of about six billion lives currently being lived on planet Earth. Many of those lives are just as busy as yours, but they are full of physical and emotional pain, the easing of which is complicated by meager resources.

In terms of the even bigger spiritual picture, being of service to others is one of the highest and brightest uses of your energy and attention. Supporting and comforting another human being helps to heal that person's heart and open yours. It also expands your awareness and helps you put the priorities of your own life in perspective.

Opportunities to be of service to those less fortunate undoubtedly exist within a one mile radius of where you live or work. Perhaps a child needs help learning to read. An elderly person might need a ride to the doctor's. A family might need groceries. Or perhaps someone just needs a friendly phone call.

If your heart is big and brave, volunteer at a Hospice or AIDS clinic. If your heart is not big and brave, volunteer, and it will be.

Earth itself is a living being who needs your care. Her skies, seas, rivers, forests, animals, dolphins, and birds are besieged; they need your protection.

If you don't have time to personally be of service to others, let your wallet do the giving. At least once a month, donate a percentage of your income to someone you know who is in need, or to a worthwhile local or national charity.

Always give service with a smile in your heart. The positive energy of every act of service ripples out, uplifting those around you, and also the planet.

POWER NAPS

Remember how resistant you were to taking naps when you were a child? Your world was new and exciting, and you didn't want to miss any of it. If, as they say, youth is wasted on the young, so are naps. Now that you are an adult, and your world is complicated and stressful, you have earned the right to nap. Even if you don't actually sleep, your body and mind can regroup and recharge.

It is neither childish nor weak to rest. Benjamin Franklin said, "He that can take rest is greater than he that can take cities." Nap as needed; there are no rules. Engineer Buckminster Fuller was against sleeping for eight hours straight, because he felt he slept a third of his life away. His solution was to sleep for half an hour every six hours, giving him twenty-two hours a day to think.

Don't worry that you might enjoy your nap so much you won't wake up in time to make a business meeting or pick your child up at school. Set an alarm to wake you up in fifteen or thirty minutes.

Take off your jacket and shoes. Loosen your tie, scarf, or belt. Depending on where you are, stretch out on a bed, sofa, the floor, or the seat of your car. If possible, put a pillow, cushion, or briefcase under your feet to get them higher than your head. This takes the pressure off your feet and helps increase the flow of blood to your upper torso and brain, refreshing the cells.

Listening to peaceful instrumental music or an inspirational meditation tape is fine. Close your eyes. Take two or three deep breaths all the way down into your belly. Focus on the rhythm of your breathing and the beat of your heart. Let thoughts pass by without following them. Relax. Be still. Just be.

Give yourself permission to nap—write yourself a note if you have to.

INCENSE SENSE

MANY spiritual and religious rites around the world use some form of incense as part of their ceremonies. Among them are the Catholic Church, the high Episcopal church, Buddhists, Hindus, Native Americans, and shamans.

They use incense not just because it smells good, but because incense is emotionally and spiritually powerful. The aroma stimulates the limbic region of our brains, the area linked to our emotions and emotional memories. You have undoubtedly experienced this effect when you have smelled cookies baking and felt warm and cared for, or were transported back to your mother's or grandmother's kitchen. Incense used for sacred purposes is of high quality, and its aroma is designed to transport you to peace and stimulate spiritual love.

The high vibrations of sacred incense also serve to raise energy levels and clear negative energy. Tibetan temple incense can be a combination of as many as fifty hand-ground herbs, spices, gems, and other ingredients. It is formulated to purify the atmosphere of worry, sadness, and discomfort. Native American healers use sage smoke to "smudge" people, driving away stress, grief, unbalanced energy, and negative spirits. They also smudge their homes and places of ritual. Once the negative energy is cleared, they might burn cedar to attract positive energy. Cedar is also said to reduce fear and calm anger. Nag Champa incense from India is effective in creating rapport around you and in your home. Lavender clears thinking and reduces stress.

Experiment with different kinds of incense in different circumstances to see how the various aromas make you feel. You do not have to be religious or spiritual for incense to work, but uplifting your energy is always beneficial.

FEARLESS

WHENEVER fear is present within you, it means you have become disconnected from power and love, because if you were connected you would not feel afraid. Fear creates a vicious circle. It immobilizes you so you are unable to take positive action. Not taking action—which is the life blood of power—makes you more frightened, which makes you feel even more paralyzed. Fear may start out as an ice cube in your heart or stomach, then it becomes bigger and colder, until it is a huge block of ice that encases you, distorts your view of the world, and freezes you out of life.

To melt the ice and break free of fear, take whatever physical, mental, emotional, or spiritual action you can. Don't put pressure on yourself to take a huge step right off the bat, because you might be afraid you can't do it, and will be in even worse shape. Take small, manageable steps that lead to bigger ones.

- Picture bright white light surrounding you and filling you from head to toe. Light is more powerful than fear, so ask it to help dissolve your fear.
- Ask your higher forces for strength and guidance.
- Breathe deeply, focusing on each breath, to connect you with the power of life and the Creator. Imagine your fear riding out on your exhalation and going into the light to be healed.
- Whistle, hum, or sing a happy tune. The sound vibrations raise your energy and disperse negative frequencies.
- The opposite of being afraid is being confident. Remember a time when you felt especially confident, to rekindle that feeling.

As your actions melt your fear you will feel stronger, more alive, brighter, and more optimistic. Fearless, you are ready to take bigger steps.

RITUAL

$\mathbf{A}$ ritual is a pre-established series of actions and sounds that direct the energy of your body, mind, emotions, and spirit toward a specific intent. Every religion has created ceremonies for such purposes as praising the Creator, giving thanks, petitioning for help, and commemorating life-altering events such as birth, passage into adulthood, marriage, and death.

Whether you are religious or spiritual or neither, you can design your own special rituals. You might want to create rites to greet the day or the night, initiate an important action, celebrate achieving a goal, honor the day of your birth, or for protection on a journey (physical or otherwise), clarity of vision, healing, or any other significant event that takes place in your life.

Be they simple or complex, the more the activities in your ritual engage each of your physical senses, the more power you impart to your objective. You can stimulate your body with rhythmic breathing, cleansing heat and water, or with motion, such as the whirling done by the Sufis, or the repetitive foot steps and hand motions in ceremonial tribal dances. Sound plays a key role because its frequencies affect your brain waves. Rattles and drums are effective, as are flutes, light music, and chanting. To stir the emotional area of your brain, light incense or put aromatic oils on your skin. The energy of the colors and objects you look at also affect your energy, as does whatever you hold. You might focus on a fire, candle, or picture, or hold a crystal, amulet, or other power object.

With your mind focused on your purpose, and the intensity of your actions arousing your energy, a ritual helps you open direct lines of communication with your subconscious and supraconscious selves, and with the Creator.

REAL WEALTH

WHAT does it mean to be really wealthy? If the answers that come to mind have to do with money, status, houses, cars, stocks, clothes, jewelry, or art, they are answers with limited possibilities.

There's nothing wrong with having material possessions, but they are tools not goals, their purpose being to provide you with freedom, comfort, and flexibility. If you use them to feel superior to others, then your negative ego is in charge of them. Because your negative ego doesn't want you to be truly wealthy, successful, or powerful, in all likelihood it will use any attachment you have to possessions to trip you up and make you fall somewhere down the road.

Looking only at material goods for your wealth is like looking at a light bulb for the light of the Creator. Look to your heart instead. Real wealth is found in having love for yourself, others, the planet, and the Creator. You can take this gold to the spiritual bank any day of your life. That's also true for kindness, integrity, empathy, generosity, loyalty, compassion, creativity, wisdom, and willpower.

Marvel at *all* the wealth you have—earth, air, water, food, sun, clothes, shelter, love, laughter, friendships, income, rest, health, knowledge, pets, stars, music, books, tools, trees, and the Creator of it all. If you begin to lament what you do not have, immediately focus on two positive things you do have. They can range from having someone in your life whom you love and who loves you, to how nice it is to turn on the faucet and have water come out.

A wondrous thing happens when you delight in how really wealthy you already are, more and more of what you want and need flows to you.

MAKE IT FLOW

Some days life just doesn't seem to flow smoothly. Your body might feel as if you have cement for blood, and your mind seems to have taken a trip to Siberia. Or maybe you're bogged down in a personal or business relationship, or conflicts and delays have derailed your work.

When the events of life aren't flowing well, the tendency is to focus on what's stuck. This is natural, but not helpful. Energy follows focus, so constantly focusing on what isn't working only exacerbates the problem. Your subconscious mind thinks you want to be stuck because that's what you're focusing on. Here's a simple trick to remind your mind that things *are* flowing.

As you move through your day, notice everything liquid that's flowing. The water flowing out of the spigot when you brush your teeth or wash your hands. The flow of the juice, tea, coffee, or water you pour yourself. The blood in your veins. Rain. A fountain. A stream.

Each time you notice something that's flowing, say to yourself, silently or aloud, "My life is flowing smoothly." Repeat it three times: once for your conscious mind, once for your subconscious, and once for your high conscious. That way the three primary dimensions of your mind are aligned with the same concept. (When flushing a toilet, imagine that anything wasteful in your life is being eliminated and flushed away.)

By dropping the idea of flowing into your thoughts like a round stone dropped in a lake, the flowing energy will ripple out into every aspect of your life. You'll find that events begin to open up and move in your favor.

HIGH SELF

IMAGINE that you are in a meadow vibrant with colorful flowers, especially red, orange, and yellow ones. On the other side of the meadow a mountain rises up into violet clouds that encircle its peak. Cross the meadow to the foot of the mountain, allowing your progress to be smooth and easy.

The base of the mountain is carpeted in emerald green grass. Rest for a moment, and imagine that you are standing in the middle of a bubble of bright white light. The light tells you that you have everything you need to get to the top of the mountain—your mind, heart, and spirit—and it will guide you. Moving with the light, you effortlessly traverse the mountain from left to right, then left again. You are almost to the top when you see a lake with clear indigo-blue water. You cannot resist taking a quick dip.

Feeling refreshed and calm, you and the light easily cover the last traverse to the top of the mountain, where you are enveloped in softly scented violet mists. On a clear crystal bench sits an old man or old woman. This is your high self, who oversees the development of your spirit and holds the love and light of the Creator for you. Your high self beckons you to sit with him or her. You do so, and when you look into your high self's eyes, you see the boundless compassion and wisdom of the Divine Power. Your high self waits for you to speak. Ask for wisdom, guidance, and healing as you travel your spiritual path on earth. Your high self bends his or her forehead to yours, and the connection feels electric with the grace of love. You sense and see all that your high self wants you to know at this time. Your spirit remembers how it feels to be home. Your high self gives you a gift, and you give your gratitude. When the connection is over, you find yourself back in the meadow at the speed of thought.

ANGER IS ELEMENTAL

CHANCES are good that you will feel angry at least once in your life. Even the Dalai Lama and the Pope have probably been angry. Being angry does not make you a bad person, because you are not your anger. It is how you handle your anger that determines how negative or positive it is.

Anger can flare up when an event occurs that hurts you or someone you love. It often seems safer to feel angry than sad. You may also feel powerless to do anything about the event that caused the hurt, and so you turn to anger, thinking it is a source of power, because you can wield your anger like a weapon and have impact. The truth is that using anger to hurt yourself or others actually transfers your true power to the anger, leaving you even more powerless.

Think of anger as being like the element of fire. It ignites, is hot, and can burn you and others. Repeatedly thinking about the harm done to you and the punishment you want to inflict, is like the wind fanning the flames higher. Focus instead on what you're really feeling. Go beneath the anger and honor the initial hurt by naming it—"I feel hurt, disappointed, diminished,"—and *feeling* it. Experiencing the sadness is equivalent to throwing water on the fire. Try using the earth to smother flames. Go for a run, a brisk walk, or a swim. Dig in the garden. Climb a tree or a rock. It's difficult to be angry when you're grounded.

Anger looks for opportunities to express itself, because, like fire, it needs fuel to exist. Extinguishing anger in a healthy way—without harm to you, another, or property—transforms the energy into a positive force that helps you take constructive action. When the flames of anger die down, your power rises up.

YOUR KIND OF SUCCESS

At a gathering on Martha's Vineyard one splendid summer evening, men and women who were nationally and internationally successful in the arts, politics, or finance, were asked what quality they valued most in a person. Without hesitation, and without exception, they answered, "Kindness."

At a time when humankind seems to have become less kind, the group's answer was heartening. As defined by *Webster's Dictionary*, being kind means: "of a sympathetic or generous nature: disposed to be helpful and solicitous: affectionate, loving: gentle." These very same adjectives can be used to define a genuinely powerful person, because true power is kind. Acts of kindness are especially empowering for both the doer and the recipient because they connect each person to his or her spiritual self, which is the real source of power.

True kindness seeks no material or ego gain. To avoid binding your kindness with the strings of hidden expectations or needs, first and foremost be helpful, sympathetic, loving, gentle, and generous with yourself. The person who is well fed and strong is better equipped to feed others.

True kindness comes from the heart and does not discriminate as to who is deserving. Be kind to everyone, at every opportunity, every day. Be kind on every level: physically, mentally, emotionally, and spiritually. Be kind particularly when it is difficult. Be helpful to children. Be sympathetic to animals. Be gentle with the earth. Be loving with your Creator. Be generously kind to yourself.

True wealth accumulates by spending the currency of kind acts. When all is said and done, here and in the hereafter, it may turn out that the success that counts is how well you have succeeded at being kind.

MORE IS MORE

Some people subscribe to the less-is-more philosophy, and in some areas of life, such as architecture, it often applies. In other areas of life, however, such as how you treat yourself, others, your work, the earth, and the Creator, the less-is-more approach can too easily turn into less-is-less.

Treat yourself with more and more respect and kindness. If lack of self-esteem makes this difficult, make a list of ten or more of your positive qualities, beginning with the phrases: "I am . . . ," "I have . . . ," or "I do. . . ." Include physical, mental, emotional, and spiritual qualities, then post the list on your mirror.

Treat others with the same respect and kindness with which you want to be treated. Share yourself and what you have. Choose someone you know and devote half an hour, half a day, a day, to helping that person in ways he or she needs. Do things that person wants to do. Performing this service sincerely, with cheer and generosity, is a gift to the person, yourself, and the Creator.

To the extent possible, do work you love, or find things to love about the work you do. Instead of doing the minimum required, invest your best efforts in your work. This approach reduces stress and anxiety and increases both the quantity and quality of your energy, which leads to increased success.

The bounty of the Earth exemplifies the more-is-more approach to life. She is your supportive friend, your nourishing mother, your inspiring mentor. Without her abundance you would be homeless and hungry. Love and respect her. Keep the Earth's lands and waters clean. Plant trees. Be kind to animals.

The more you participate in the divine dance of life by giving your best to yourself, others, your work, and the Earth, the fuller and richer your life will be.

FOOD BLESSINGS

"**R**UB-A-DUB-DUB, thanks for the grub. Yea God!" The blessing is short and fun, but it gets the job done. It contains the two basic components of blessing food: acknowledging the gift of food, and giving thanks to the Creator.

Food is a blessing and a miracle. In its original form it contains the spark of life given to all living things by the Creator, and as it grows it becomes a synthesis of energy of the four elements: earth, sun, air, and water. When you eat, that energy becomes part of your body, nourishing you so you can live, work, play, learn, and love. Color therapists say that even the colors of food stimulate energy centers in the body. The further removed food is from the Earth, and the more it is changed, the more power it loses and the less power you gain. The quality of the food you choose to eat can reflect how distant you want to be from the power of the Earth and the Creator, or how close.

Whether you are going to eat beans or ribs, a carrot or a cupcake, bless your food before you eat it. It helps focus your attention on what you are doing. It makes you more aware that food connects you directly with the power of the Creator and the Earth. It reminds you of the many ways the Creator nourishes you. It gives you an opportunity to be grateful for the bountiful gifts the Creator and the Earth provide. Blessing food also helps eliminate negative energy from the food and endows it with positive energy. Raising the vibration of your food will then raise your vibration, and it might even help make food more digestible. You can also affirm the positive ways you will use the energy you have received.

It is more important that your words be heartfelt than eloquent. When you bless your food, it then blesses you, connecting you with the circle of life.

EMOTIONAL CENTER

Your emotions may turn out to be the strongest links in the chain of life. It is important to respect all of them; the good, the bad, and the ugly.

Regrettably, it is possible—even probable—that into your life some pain may fall. When it does, the tendency is to avoid dealing with the pain because it falls into the bad *and* the ugly categories. Unfortunately, avoidance does not make pain disappear, and usually causes it to intensify. Not coping with pain is like ignoring a leaking pipe, pretty soon you are awash in pain.

Pasting a smile over your pain and pretending it isn't there only works for the short term. Distracting yourself from it by working, exercising, eating, or drinking excessively, only delays the moment of truth. Whether it is days or years from now, your higher self will eventually force you to face your pain to help you heal and grow, because when you're truly free of pain, you are more free to love.

Instead of prolonging the agony, take charge of your pain. Choose to face it. Sit quietly with your eyes closed. Locate where in your body the emotional pain feels the most intense. It might be your heart, solar plexus, stomach, or mind. The area might physically hurt or feel tight. Or you might intuitively sense where the pain is lodged.

Zoom your attention right into the center of the pain, like a pain-seeking missile. Let it explode in tears, or sobs, or yells. If you feel like pounding your fists, pick something that won't hurt you or it, like a pillow or a cushioned chair.

A funny thing happens on the way to the center of your pain—it disappears. Instead of pain you will feel a deep sense of relief, strength, peace, and expansive lightness.

FILLING UP

You want to improve yourself and your life by letting go of habits that do not further you. Maybe you are trying to stop being critical or angry. You might want to be less timid at work, or less forgetful of people's names. Cutting down on eating sugar or using swear words would be good. But how long do your well-intended changes last? Does it seem that for every foot you gain, you slide back two? The emptiness syndrome could be at work.

What often happens when you eliminate something negative is that it creates an emptiness. The part of you that is used to having that negative habit around experiences the change as loss and does not like the feeling. The emptiness looks around for something to fill it. The closest, most convenient candidate is the very habit you are trying to release. The emptiness pulls the negative habit back into itself and holds on to it even more tightly so as not to lose it again. The emptiness does not care what it fills itself with, it only cares that it is full.

Whenever you let go of something, fill the space with something positive. Take a moment to become aware of your body by being quiet and breathing deeply a few times. Sense where in your body the habit lived: heart, head, stomach, back, or right knee. Imagine the space like an empty bowl. What size and color is it? Fill the bowl with bright white light. Then create a mental image of you behaving in the new, improved way, and put that into the bowl.

Match your physical actions to the new mental images: be complimentary, remain calm, go after what you need at work, remember people's names, eat sugarless foods, make up nonswear swear words. Change can be fulfilling.

INTERIOR DESIGNS

How would you describe where you live? Is the structure solid or drafty? Are the rooms bright and airy, or dim and stale? Is it tidy or messy? Clean or grimy? Is your furniture comfortable or for show? Are visitors welcome?

We have come to think of the various aspects of our lives as being separate, but actually everything is connected. By understanding one part we gain understanding of another part. An old proverb says, "If you understand a grain of sand, you understand the universe."

Your home is indeed your castle; it is also a reflection of your inner self. A solid home reflects a strong sense of self. Bright, airy rooms reflect someone with positive thoughts, open to fresh ideas. Dark, closed rooms can mean that dark thoughts dominate. Clutter might indicate scattered thinking, or creative right-brain activity. Too much organization—those alphabetized soups—reveals rigid, inflexible emotions or excessive left-brain thinking. Unused items crowding closets are outmoded beliefs or attachments to the past. Uncomfortable, showy furniture might mean that you are not comfortable with yourself and put on a show to disguise the fact. Dirty windows distort your view of the outside world. Visitors represent different ideas and points of view you are willing to entertain.

You get the idea. Fortunately, because everything is connected, by changing the interior design of your home you can change the design of your interior. Trade drab colors for bright. Fill in drafty gaps. Clear out closets and cupboards, donating items to a homeless or battered women's shelter. Clean and open windows. Organize your papers. Mix up those soups. Buy big comfortable pillows. Put out the welcome mat. You're right at home.

REVVING UP

ALL your systems of energy—body, mind, heart, and spirit—are connected, so activity in one area affects all the other areas. Your physical body is a storehouse of energy, with each of its trillions and trillions of vibrating molecules generating energy for you to use in your physical and nonphysical endeavors.

To rev up that energy and get it circulating, exercise your body. If all you can do is take a walk, do that, but do it as briskly as possible. Being outdoors in the sunshine and the fresh air also allows you to breathe in the life force in the air, sometimes called prana, chi, or mana. Gentle swimming is another exercise that is easy to do if you have physical limitations, because the water buoys you.

If you are physically capable of doing more than walking or swimming, go for it. Run, rock climb, climb trees, jump rope, skip, work out, hike, paddle a canoe, row a boat, hopscotch, do gymnastics or ballet, ride a horse, or skate. Doing Yoga, an ancient system of postures from India, strengthens and harmonizes your body within itself, and also with your mind and spirit. Walking on your hands and feet like a lion shifts the pull of gravity on your organs, decreases tension, increases circulation, and limbers up your muscles. The more fun your exercise of choice is, the more you energize not only your body, but your thoughts, emotions, and spirit.

Engaging in exercise activities that involve other people has a synergistic effect because your energy and theirs combine to generate greater energy. Play sports such as tennis, basketball, baseball, soccer, football, water polo, or volleyball. Play badminton or Ping-Pong. Go sailing or dancing with someone.

The more you enjoy exercising, the more you will enjoy life, and for longer.

NATURAL POWER

NATURE is powerful. This is hardly a news flash, but more and more people are more and more removed from nature. This separation is due in large part to urban living and the expansion of technology, which make it easier for people to be in touch with their computer keyboards than with flowers and stones.

In addition, millions of people around the globe have been embroiled in a power struggle with nature for the last three hundred years, treating the earth as if it were the enemy. Trying to tame nature, instead of working with it, is like trying to tame the Creator who created it, and is ultimately an effort in futility.

The truth is that the birds, flowers, rivers, and clouds live in closer harmony with the Creator than most of humankind. When we separate ourselves from nature we separate ourselves from the Creator and from our core selves. This in turn causes us to be disconnected from the source of power.

Connect with nature as often as you can. Play in a park. Walk barefoot on the Earth. Talk to a robin. Visit a botanical garden. Plant a tree. Feel the sun. Go for a swim in an ocean, lake, or river. Feel a breeze. A pre-Mao Chinese gentleman had his gardener bring him a bowl of fresh earth every morning that he would smell deeply to invigorate his body, mind, and spirit.

Nature teaches you about yourself and the world, and the power that created you and your world. Look for the seasons of nature in life, projects, and relationships. Really see a tree or the sea and consider what they symbolize. Contemplate the air, the sun. Watch the cooperation of ants. Be inspired by the bee who is aerodynamically unsuited for flying but doesn't know it. Being in touch with nature puts you in touch with your true nature. This is true power.

DEAR BODY

W HEN your body hurts, is ill, or is impaired in any way, it is vital to love the part that has lost its harmony. Sometimes the tendency is to be impatient, even angry with your body for not working properly, but such negative energy obstructs the natural healing forces at work, making the situation worse and delaying recovery.

Your body wants to be healthy. That is its natural, desired state. Every atom and molecule of every cell in your body is conscious, and is influenced by the energy of your thoughts and feelings. If that energy is low and harsh, it impedes the cells' efforts to regain balance, stability, and health. You would not physically hit the part of your body that hurts, so it makes sense not to hit it emotionally or mentally. Loving, positive mental and emotional energy supports your cells' attempts to be in harmony with each other, you, and the Creator.

To expedite the healing process on the nonphysical levels, write your body a love letter. Or, if you would rather sing your body a love song, do that. Begin, "Dear Body," then tell it how much you appreciate all that it does for you. Mention how well it facilitates you moving around on the physical plane. Then address each area of your body that is in distress. Tell it you love it. Describe how much you need it and why. Thank it for all the years of service it has given you twenty-four hours a day. Apologize for allowing it to be hurt. Tell it that you are surrounding and filling the area with bright white light to protect it, cleanse it, absorb pain, and nourish it on all levels. Visualize the light there. Tell the area how happy you will be when it is strong and healthy again, and visualize that happening. Your body is dear to you. Let it know.

SPIRITUAL UNION

WHAT do jumbo shrimp and spiritual ego have in common? They are both oxymorons, because the words contradict one another.

People who take pride in being religious or spiritual, sometimes expand their negative egos instead of their loving spirits. They compare their righteousness to yours and find it superior. They let you know that the path they have chosen is not only the better path, but the only path. Where they will be saved, you, poor misguided and unenlightened wretch, are doomed. They even project their egocentricity onto their God-Goddess-Messiah-Emancipator-Savior-Leader-Guru, declaring that He, She, or It, is the one and only One and Only.

Such attitudes are totally at odds with the we-are-all-one spirit of spirituality. They are the postures of collective negative egos run amok in the ultimate playing field. It is perhaps also an ultimate irony that your negative ego, in its quest to claim the grail of superior, judgmental, manipulative, destructive power for itself, damns you to the hell of being separated from the joy of true spirit.

Where is the compassion in superiority? Where is the mercy in judgment? Where is the love in exclusivity? The Force that creates you, the world, and the universe, creates boundless variety, which It loves equally and fully. It does not love the pine tree more than the tamarind, nor the bear more than the beetle. It does not love blue eyes and white skin more than brown eyes and brown skin. It does not love Christians more than Jews. It does not love the sun more than it loves the moon. If the Force loves all life, who are we not to?

In the infinite heart of the Creator, you are unique, but you are neither more special than another, nor separate. The spiritual union is open to all. Join.

RECLAIMING POWER

At birth we bring with us all the power we will need to lovingly and successfully live our entire lives. Much of our time on earth is then spent learning how to incorporate our Creator-given power into our physical lives. The teachers and classrooms change, but the lessons remain essentially the same: how to use personal power effectively for good.

If a particular aspect of your life is not going well—chronic or severe illness, conflicted relationships, disappearing success, or money woes—this can be an indication that you have given some of your power away. You might have given it to a parent, a teacher, a lover, a friend, or a business partner. You might have been a child, an adolescent, or an adult when you did it.

The three basic reasons you give your power away are:

1. You thought it would help someone.

2. You believed that giving away what was precious to you would make the other person love you or need you.

3. Someone wanted your power and you gave it to them, or you didn't know how to prevent them from taking it.

To reclaim your power, visualize the person you might have given your power to. Looking into their eyes ask if they have any of your power. If they say yes, ask them to return it to you. If they resist, ask why they don't want to return it. Their answer can be revealing. Insist that they return your power until they do. They will hold your power out to you in symbolic form, perhaps as a ball of white light, a crystal, a sword, or other bright object. Reach out and take your power back into your own hands. Feel the energy of it. Ask it where in your body it wants to return to, and place it there, breathing it in. Repeat these steps with other people you have known until you feel full of power.

THE BREATH CONNECTION

WHENEVER you feel tense, angry, hurt, or frightened, check your breathing. In all probability it is shallow and tight. You might even be holding your breath.

Because your breathing serves to connect you with yourself and your feelings, not breathing fully is an unconscious defense mechanism for disconnecting from unpleasant emotions you would rather not experience. Shallow breathing can lessen how much of your emotions you feel, but suppressing them does not eliminate them, instead it puts your emotions in a pressure cooker. The more you inhibit the release of your emotions, the more the pressure builds in unhealthy ways in your body, mind, and heart.

Not breathing fully also disconnects you from your power. Breath is life, and the Chinese believe that your vital energy, or chi, is seated in your belly. When your breathing is shallow, it is not strong enough to activate the power in your belly, so you are unable to take positive action in the situation that caused the difficult emotions. The chicken or the egg question is whether you were already disconnected from your power, which made you afraid to feel your feelings, or whether your fear is what cut you off from your power.

Fortunately, your breath is also the switch by which you can turn on your power. When you realize your breathing is shallow, begin taking deep, even breaths. With every inhalation, mentally reinforce that you are connecting with your power. With every exhalation, allow the release of emotional tension.

When the waves of your energy become strong and calm, others involved in the situation sense it and respond more positively to you. Making the breath connection helps you promote the healing and resolution of problems.

EMOTIONAL SHAPE

EMOTIONS—love, pain, anger, peace, fear, jealousy, joy—are tricky. They're all energy. Abstract. Always changing and on the move. Just when you think you've grabbed hold of one, it squeezes out of your grasp like a wet bar of soap.

Trying to separate from your emotions because they feel uncomfortably powerful does not work. We were given both a mind and a heart so they could work synergistically, producing greater effects together than either one by itself.

Use your head to get a handle on your emotional heart by drawing pictures of your emotions. Drawing a feeling means giving it shape, color, and relative size. Once an emotion has form, it is much easier to understand and take charge of, otherwise it can be like trying to pour the wind into a glass.

Gather a few large sheets of plain paper and colored crayons or markers. Pick your favorite color and draw about a three inch diameter circle in the middle of the paper to represent you. Breathe deeply, becoming aware of where you feel the emotion in your body. Chest? Stomach? Solar plexus? Focus on the feeling. How does it feel physically? Tight? Open? Warm? Cool?

Observe your emotion without judging it. What color is it? Choose that color marker. What shape is your emotion? Round? Angular? Swirly? Square? Blobby? Draw the emotion and color in any other details.

Is it bigger or smaller than you? If it is an unpleasant emotion, and bigger than you, draw a second picture making the emotion smaller than you, or nonexistent, to give yourself the message that you are in charge of it. To reinforce positive emotions, post pictures of them where you can see them. Your emotional life shapes up when you give emotions shape.

SAY SO

Wнεн you tell a computer what to do, the command needs to be clear and accurate because the computer does not second guess you. The same holds true when you tell your subconscious mind what it is you want, because it takes everything you say literally: What you say programs it to produce that result.

Affirmations are made for this. Create a statement that describes your goal. Keep it short, simple, and declarative. Make it positive, because you do not want any negative words in the mix. Include a positive emotion verb so the affirmation activates both heart and mind. Phrase it in the present tense, because to your subconscious all time is the present. For example, "I enjoy excellent health in body, mind, and heart." "I love having money come to me beautifully and bountifully." "I love having love in my life every day."

Affirmations get the attention of your subconscious through repetition and emotional intensity. Repeat your affirmation often. Write it out a hundred times. Post the sheets of paper in different places— mirror, refrigerator, closet door—so that whenever you see them you and your subconscious are reminded of your goal. Say or sing your affirmation ten times in a row, several times a day. This is a great way to use your time when you are stopped at a red light, waiting for an elevator, standing in line, or are on hold on the telephone.

When you repeat your affirmation, don't do it hurriedly and mechanically to get it over with. If you do, you communicate that rushed, tense energy to your subconscious along with the words, and it will think you want your goal to be full of tension and over in a hurry. Energize each statement you write or say by putting your attention and delight into it. Giving it your say so makes it so!

SING YOUR NAME

Do you want to start the day off on a positive note? Sing your name as you're getting ready in the morning. The sound of your name has power and arouses your spirit. Even just saying your name a few times will help bring you into fuller consciousness so you can be more alert and aware throughout the day. Singing helps brush the cobwebs from your mind, flexes your energy, and turns the light on in your heart.

It doesn't matter if you're a total monotone, a shower only singer, or trained in opera, have fun with it. You can sing your name to a melody you know, or to one you improvise. Try rhyming your name with other words, but be sure they're positive. Be playful.

Once you've warmed up your name with song, think of a simple, present tense affirmation for something you want to have, or do, or be. Then create a song of power about your goal. It imprints on your subconscious better if the words rhyme, but don't worry if they don't scan. For example, you might sing:

"Money (or joy, love, success, health) flows to me abundantly and continually."
"I am healthy, wealthy, and wise, in every way I can devise."
"I share love and light, every day in every way, keeping myself and others bright."

Try different tunes and combinations. Sometimes the rhythm of the words themselves will suggest a melody.

When you combine your name with goals in a song, you begin the day in harmony, with fortissimo.

ALIVE AND AWARE

THE more aware you are, the more alive you are, and the more alive you are, the more aware you are. The following experience stimulates both your awareness and your sense of aliveness.

In your favorite room, gather these materials: something that smells great such as fragrant flowers, incense, or herbal tea; instrumental music that moves your spirit; an object with a distinctive texture such as a shell, a piece of velvet, or something metal; a painting or photograph of someone or something you love; and a mint or fruit-flavored pastille.

Turn off the phone, arrange not to be interrupted for fifteen minutes, and turn on the music. Light the incense, or put the flowers or tea next to where you will be seated. Sit comfortably in a chair or on a pillow, with your spine straight. Place the picture in front of you, hold the textured object, and put the pastille in your mouth. Each of your five senses—sight, sound, smell, taste, and touch—is being stimulated. Breathing fully and naturally, focus on one of your senses, then another, and so on, until you have experienced all five.

Now, try being aware of all your senses simultaneously. To see the picture, hear the music, smell the aroma, taste the flavor, and feel the texture all at the same time, stretches and alters your consciousness. It requires switching to your right brain and experiencing the present as whole, instead of fragmented. Hold your attention lightly within yourself, in a single point that becomes all points. Into this point bring your breathing, the beat of your heart, your stillness. Sense the wide-open clarity and peacefulness present within you. Be open to insights. When you enliven your awareness, you enliven your life.

INTIMATE CONVERSATION

On the list of challenging conversational topics—feelings, failures, money, sex—talking about death is probably at the head of the list. Many people are afraid of dying, afraid of death, and afraid of the unknown, making conversations about the end of physical life a triple threat.

It is these very fears that make talking about death all the more imperative, because one of the best ways to diminish fear is to meet it head on. Not talking about an event as life-altering as death does not make it go away.

Who is a good person to talk to about death? The first person you might want to talk to is yourself. How do you feel about death? Try writing five sentences describing your feelings and beliefs, or complete these phrases: "I am afraid . . . ," "I think . . . ," "I believe . . . ," "I wonder . . . ," "I want . . . ." Have you planned for death? Do you have a will? Have you obtained a living will in the event you are unable to make decisions? What do you need to die with dignity?

Once you have articulated some of your feelings about death, you will feel better equipped to talk with another person about this sensitive subject. Some good choices are: a religious counselor, a mate, a relative, a close friend, or someone who has had a near-death experience. Use your discretion when talking with someone who is dying.

Begin the discussion by saying that you have been thinking about death because it is such a meaningful event. Ask the person's permission to talk about death. Share your thoughts and feelings. Ask the person what he or she thinks and feels about death. How have they planned for it? What does the person believes happens after death?

Discussing death is one of the most intimate, rewarding, and powerful conversations you will ever have. Ironically, it is life affirming.

ANIMAL STRENGTH

ANIMALS have strong spirits because they live in deep harmony with nature and with the Creator. Native Americans and other native people throughout the world regard animals as powerful teachers, healers, messengers, and protectors. Sacred images of animals play important roles in their ceremonies, and animals add power to the healing and visions of shamans.

Over a million species of animals live on the planet. The animal kingdom includes mammals, birds, amphibians, reptiles, fish, and insects, each with a special purpose and talent. An animal might be fast, strong, smart, able to see in the dark, playful, protective, good at communicating, or loyal. By connecting with the spiritual energy of a particular animal, you connect with that animal's gifts and wisdom. You can learn from animals because nature is the Great Teacher.

The universe provides every person with the helpful spirit of one or more animals. To discover yours, take time to breathe and be still, then ask your personal power animal to make itself known to you. Over the next three days you might see pictures of a particular animal, hear about one, see an animal in a dream, or see the physical animal. Such events confirm which animal is there to help you become one with life. It could be a buffalo, lizard, hawk, moose, deer, or ant. Don't let your negative ego dismiss an animal as being unappealing.

Keep your animal ally well fed with attention, respect, and gratitude. Invite it to teach you its valuable lessons. Trust it to know what you need. Ask what *it* needs. Ask it for guidance whether you are calm or in crisis. Your power animal can show you how to live in harmony with nature, even if you live in a city. The insights you gain from your animal ally will help make you strong within yourself.

REAL RAPPORT

DISTANCE and difference do not disconnect you from others anymore than your brain is disconnected from your foot. If you stub your toe, your brain knows it, because it is wired to every part of your body through the nerve system, which relays electrical impulses to it. In a similar way, your subconscious mind is wired to everyone else's subconscious through energy and awareness.

Knowing that you know and they know means that establishing rapport with the people you know and meet is exceptionally important. If you are talking to someone and are thinking how awful they look, or how stupid and clumsy they are, those thoughts go from your conscious mind to your subconscious, to their subconscious mind, at the speed of thought. Their conscious minds may or may not be able to articulate that information—it depends on how in tune the person is with their subconscious mind—but they will certainly sense the negative energy.

The quality of your thoughts about a person affects the quality of your interactions, which affects the quality of the outcome. Negative thoughts create conflict and limitations; positive thoughts create harmony and plenty. In addition to thinking positive thoughts about family, friends, and co-workers, think positively about everyone with whom you come in contact. Be sure your intentions are also positive. If you think complimentary thoughts so you can manipulate the other person, that negative intention is communicated, too.

When providing or receiving a service, buying or selling something, if you are a healer or a patient, a teacher or a student, thinking positive thoughts about the other person will create positive results. This is real rapport!

HONESTY POLICY

To be honest means to be truthful, candid, genuine, straightforward. What is your policy regarding honesty? Are you honest all the time? Most of the time? Some of the time? Hardly ever? How honest are you about big issues? In small matters? About what you have done? About what you have not done?

A large part of being truthful means taking complete responsibility for your actions. When your actions are positive—"I washed the dishes"—honesty comes easily. But when your actions have negative impact—"I broke your favorite cup"—being honest is difficult, because you shrink from experiencing the person's hurt or anger. The more harm caused, the more challenging being honest becomes.

Lying to avoid responsibility creates discord within you, between you and those you have injured, and between you and your Creator. On subconscious and supraconscious levels everyone knows you lied. The dissonant energy between your lie and the truth reverberates through everything you think, say, feel, and do, causing your actions to become imbalanced and distorted. The friction also causes stress in your body, which can lead to illness.

The long-term, multi-level harm caused by lying is usually worse than simply dealing with the consequences of your actions. The truth frees you from discord, invigorates your character, and restores harmony with your Creator.

When faced with a situation where it is truth that could cause hurt, avoid telling a "white lie." Instead, find something to say that is both true and polite, or ask the person for permission to speak honestly, but let kindness lead your truth.

Honesty is the backbone of virtue. Without honesty, you lack integrity, which is like having a body without bones. Honesty is the best and only policy.

THE ART OF SILLY

How long has it been since you were silly? Not minding what people think. Just having fun. Loosey goosey. Enjoying yourself.

Being deliberately silly is an art. It's like poetic license; you have to learn the rules of life's rhyme and reason before you can take liberties with them. Most comedians, for instance, are well versed in the serious side of life. Most truly bright and creative people indulge in being silly. Einstein once wore Mickey Mouse ears on his head when greeting an interviewer.

This is not witless silliness, but playfulness—allowing yourself to express those impish impulses you might normally suppress for fear of what other people will think. So make a silly face. Talk in a funny, high-pitched voice. Try bantering with someone. Put something on top of your head that doesn't belong there. Make a weird sound. Do something spontaneously wacky with your body, maybe a little cha-cha-cha when you arrive home from work. The caveat, of course, is always to not harm yourself, others, or property.

If you feel too self-conscious to be silly in front of others, start out by being silly just for you. Then try it in front of your dog. Work up to people. Keep in mind that the worst that happens is that someone thinks you're silly. This will not bring your world crashing to an end, and it can even be taken as a compliment.

Silliness is a mini-vacation for your spirit. It breaks you out of the mold of your day-to-day life, allowing you to expand. It lets your child-self come out and play. You might even discover the solution to a problem, hit upon a creative way of doing something, or gain insight into yourself.

Be silly, willy nilly. Be artful—or not. Be loosey goosey, if only for a moment.

BRIGHTEN UP

COLORS are waves of energy traveling at different speeds through matter. The energy of the colors you wear, and with which you surround yourself—upholstery, sheets, walls, pillows, carpets—have an affect on many aspects of your energy. Colored light entering your eyes affects your brain waves and emotions, and can increase or decrease your physical energy.

White contains all the colors. You can see this by letting a beam of white sunlight pass through a pyramid-shaped glass prism. The prism refracts and disperses the white light into a rainbow of colors. Technically, black is not a color because it is the absence of light and so of color. The three primary colors are red, green, and blue. If you shine three lights—each a primary color—at the same spot, the place where they converge will be white. Mixing primary colors in different combinations and proportions produces any color in the spectrum.

Like the sun itself, which stimulates life, the brighter the colors you look at, the more light they have, and the more energy they stimulate. The darker the colors you look at, the less light they have, and the more they diminish energy. Wear darker or softer colors when you want to rest, and bright, strong colors when you want to be energized. Specific colors also have specific affects.

Red: Increases physical energy, improves circulation; sacrum
Orange: Helps digestion, motivates action, creativity, social; spleen
Yellow: Sharpens intellect, gives a sunny disposition; adrenal
Green: Balances heart emotions, nature, brings prosperity; heart
Blue: Peaceful, expands intuition, communication; thyroid
Indigo: Spiritual awareness, anti-inflammatory; pituitary
Violet: Increases spiritual wisdom, purifies; pineal gland

Pick the colors you need to brighten body, mind, heart, or spirit.

FREE OF FEAR

THE adventure of learning to connect with your power does not usually progress in steady increments, instead it stops and starts and sometimes seems to go sideways, even upside-down. During the times when the process is not progressing smoothly, you may experience varying degrees of fear, from mild to severe, depending on how disconnected from your power you are.

When you feel afraid, you communicate the emotional energy and images of what you fear to your subconscious mind. Your subconscious, being very literal and having limited ability to discriminate between what furthers you and what hinders you, thinks you like being afraid. Even more significantly, it thinks that you want the very thing you are afraid of to happen. Because one of the main functions of your subconscious is to manifest your thoughts in the physical world, it uses the energy of your fear as a magnet to attract to you the event you are afraid of. Voilà, that which you fear occurs. For example, if you are afraid of being bitten by a dog, you will undoubtedly be bitten by one. Likewise, if you are afraid of being robbed, abandoned, emotionally hurt, physically hurt, fired, betrayed, poor, or ill, you transmit strong images and emotions of those events to your subconscious mind, and it manifests them.

Energy follows focus. Instead of feeding your fear by focusing on what you are afraid might happen, starve your fear by focusing on the pleasant event you would like to have happen. Create a powerful, detailed, colorful mental image of you safely petting a strange dog. See yourself as happy, healthy, confident, loved, loving, prosperous, and profitably employed. Picture your possessions being intact.

When you are free of fear, you are free to be powerful.

LOVING

I T is entirely possible that a large part of the reason you enroll in life on earth is to learn to become fully loving. Just in case being more loving turns out to be a major part of your curriculum, initiate at least one loving action in every twenty-four hour period, every week, every month, every year of your life.

To be loving means being caring, warm, helpful, kind, considerate, tender, compassionate, empathetic, appreciative, and humane. Every loving action you take helps you open your heart and grow, no matter how significant or seemingly insignificant the action is. You might help a child reach a drinking fountain, forgive yourself for making a mistake, praise a friend's efforts, or save a forest.

Be loving to yourself. Your pitcher must be filled with water before you can quench another's thirst. Be loving to others—relatives, friends, and enemies. They are mirrors of yourself, part of Creation. Be loving to the Earth which loves you by nourishing and supporting you, literally and aesthetically. Love your life. Be loving to the Creator who lovingly created you and everyone and everything.

Express love through physical, mental, emotional, and spiritual action. Say prayers for people you care about, and those with whom you are in conflict. An all-purpose prayer is: "Sacred Creator and Blessed Angels, please surround (name of prayee) with light, and grace them with your love, that they are loved, helped, healed, protected and empowered, in all the ways they have need."

Think positive thoughts about people you know and meet. Visualize them achieving the success they seek, being fulfilled, and, of course, being loving.

Learning to be fully loving on all levels is a lifetime course, and helps you graduate from the need to attend Earth school.

RESPONSE-ABLE

You may be among the elite group of people who are perfect, but most of us make mistakes on a daily basis. We misunderstand what someone said, zig when we should have zagged, take our stress out on others, and forget to do things that need doing. The tricky bit is what you do afterward.

One of the key turning points in personal evolution is being willing and able to take responsibility for the negative impact of your actions. If you tend to confuse responsibility with blame, then when you do something wrong you feel flattened by the weight of self-blame and trapped in feelings of shame. These are unpowerful feelings, which prevent you from taking positive action. Yes, being responsible means to be held accountable, but the higher octave of the definition means having the power within you to respond to the negative effects of your actions in an appropriate and constructive manner.

Be actively responsible. Instead of avoiding people whom you have inconvenienced, hindered, or hurt—physically, mentally, or emotionally—seek them out and apologize. Ask how they are feeling as a result of what you did. Find out what other unpleasant events occurred because of your misguided actions. Apologize again, sincerely! Those three little words, "I am sorry," speak volumes. They say that you acknowledge what you did, accept responsibility, and that you regret your actions and the distress they caused. After clearing the emotional air, set about repairing any other harm you caused, as best you can.

Being willing to be "response-able" is what transforms a mistake into an opportunity for learning and growth. Such powerful and empowering actions will in turn produce positive responses from others.

TAKE NOTE

PEOPLE have recorded the events of their lives ever since they could, in whatever form they could. During the Ice Age, which took place approximately 60,000 to 10,000 B.C., people in Lascaux, France, painted pictures of their hunts on the walls of caves. Around 3500 B.C., the Sumerians introduced writing. About two thousand years later, the Egyptians came up with parchment.

Thanks to the innovations of the Chinese in A.D. 105, we now have paper on which to write and draw. Record the events of your life in a special notebook—it can be utilitarian or arty. Include not only physical incidents, but mental, emotional, and spiritual events as well. Write in longhand because the hand-eye-brain connection plugs you into higher-powered energy.

You might prefer writing in your journal first thing in the morning, or last thing at night, or anytime in between. Try different times to get a feel for when words flow best for you. You are free to write totally honestly because no one is going to evaluate the worth of the content but you, and no one is going to grade you on grammar and spelling. Keeping this in mind is liberating.

Write, write, write. Throw syntax to the wind. The more non-sequitors the merrier. Write everything that leaps to mind. Take note of the good, the bad, and the ugly of your feelings, thoughts, wants, and needs. Own what you did, and hope to do, the naughty and the nice. Rave against and for. Revile and glorify. Draw pictures and symbols. Ruminate on whys and wherefores.

Everything you write is from you, about you, for you. It relieves pressure, leads you to insights, and gives juice to your creativity. By writing and drawing it on the page you create a mirror that lets you see in.

LAUGH RELIEF

WHEN was the last time you laughed? Remember how good it felt? How it made you feel open and loose. How you felt whole and alive, connected to yourself and in harmony with life.

Laughter feels good all over and is good for you. It is indeed one of the best medicines. Laughter releases tension and reduces stress. It stimulates the immune system. Research at Loma Linda University in California showed that when a person laughs, the body produces more cells that kill infection. Belly laughs help improve digestion. Author Norman Cousins credited laughter with boosting the quality of his health when he was undergoing medical treatment.

People all over the world know that laughing benefits them. An Italian proverb says, "Laughter makes good blood." An Irish proverb says, "A good laugh and a long sleep are the best cures in the doctor's book." A group in India formed a laughter club where the members get together just to laugh.

Laughing is infectious because its lighthearted energy sets off a chain reaction. It opens your heart to other positive emotions. The joy sparked by laughing also lifts you closer to the hearts of angels and the Creator.

You may laugh with others, but not at them. Other than that caveat, go for the laugh. Dare to be silly. Watch funny movies, television programs, and cartoons. Read humorous books. Go to comedy clubs. Look for the humor in life, because ten years from now the goofs won't seem so serious. The gap between what is and what was meant to be can often be hilarious. If you are wise, you will laugh at yourself. Laugh fully and long every day. Anthony Burgess said, "Laugh and the world laughs with you; snore and you sleep alone."

SUCCESS JUICE

JUST as a light bulb needs electricity to light up, success needs emotional energy to be bright. Here are three ways to turn on the success juice.

1. Think about a success you have achieved in the past, really putting your heart into the memory of it. Re-experience the satisfaction and elation you felt, and how happy you were with yourself and the world to have achieved your goal. Cranking up the positive emotions associated with your past successes reinforces your love of success to your subconscious mind, programming it to help you create success for other goals you are working toward.

2. How do you react when other people succeed? Do you feel jealous? If you resent other people's success, you are communicating two negative attitudes to your subconscious: You don't like success and success is so scarce there isn't enough to go around for both others and you to succeed. Keep in mind that the people you know are reflections of facets of yourself. When they succeed, it means you succeed. Congratulate them. Be glad. Be inspired. Celebrate others' success and you will have more occasions to celebrate your own.

3. Create a mental picture of how you will look being successful, then mentally walk into the picture, experiencing the excitement of your success as if it were happening now. Infusing the mental image of success with joy gets the attention of your subconscious, which begins to mobilize its forces to bring you the people, information, resources, and opportunities you need to succeed.

One-two-three, generating positive past, present, and future emotional juice helps you manifest your goals successfully and brightly.

ADOLESCENT

Every experience you have is alive in your subconscious mind in living color and emotion. This means that your adolescent self is alive, and perhaps not too well, in the realm of your subconscious. The energy of any pain or fear that your adolescent is experiencing, can affect the energy and events of the reality you are currently focusing on in your adult experience.

You can get in touch with your adolescent self through visualization. Sit in a chair that supports your back, and take three deep breaths. On the last deep inhalation call up a mental image of yourself as a teenager. Take a good mental look at yourself. What are you wearing? How is your hair cut? What is your adolescent self doing and where? What is your mood?

Do you see anything about you then that reminds you of you now? How do you feel toward your adolescent self? Angry? Forgiving? Impatient? Loving? You can create more compassion for yourself at that age through understanding. Adolescence is a very tricky stage. You enter new levels of awareness and power. In the Jewish tradition, the age of thirteen is regarded as the time when the soul becomes fully integrated with the physical body. You are more aware of yourself as a person, and also more vulnerable to how others perceive you.

All this growing awareness calls for your love and support. Speak to your adolescent self as a friend. Tell them you love them and are there for them. Ask them how they are feeling. Listen without judgment. Kindly offer what wisdom you have learned as an adult. Ask them what they need and want. Give it to them, then give them a big hug and surround them with white light. The love you give your adolescent self will help raise their energy, which will help raise yours.

SMUDGING

NATIVE American medicine people practice a purification ritual known as "smudging." When someone is experiencing physical or mental distress, or a family or business crisis, the events are seen as symptoms of an imbalance in the person's energy field. The imbalance can be caused by unproductive thinking or emotions, or a negative or lost spirit that has attached itself to the person. Smudging the person with the smoke from smoldering dried sage helps cleanse his or her energy of negativity and restores balance.

You may not be connected with a Native American healer, but you can still achieve excellent benefits by doing the smudging yourself. Sage, loose or bound into sticks, can be found in health food, Native American, and New Age stores. Put the sage in an abalone shell or fireproof bowl and light it. Fan the flames out using a feather or your hand, so the sage smolders.

Hold the bowl of sage up in front of you, toward Father Sky, saying in your own words or these, "Great Spirit I thank you for this gift of sage. I offer this sacred smoke to you, and respectfully ask you to bless it, that it in turn blesses me in all the ways I have need." Offer the sage to each of the four directions, turning sunward, or clockwise. Give permission for your problem to be released by the smoke into the Light, and open a door or a window for it to leave through.

Holding the pot of smoldering sage with two hands, pass it from your head to your feet, and from side to side. Then place it safely on the floor and turn slowly just in front of it to surround yourself with the rising sacred smoke. Repeat your desire to be cleansed and balanced. You will begin to feel clearer, lighter, and smoother. Give thanks to the Great Spirit and to the spirit of the sage.

REALITY CHECK

Rumors, gossip, and prophecies abound regarding cataclysmic earth changes to come. If you are not too fond of yourself or your life, you may be among those who believe the horrors you hear. The more you give your power to the belief, the more likely you are to experience devastation, because energy pours into whatever you focus on and manifests it. However—and it is a huge however—you have the power to choose what reality you experience.

Physicists now agree with metaphysicists that every thought manifests in some layer or bubble of the universe, creating an infinite variety of possible realities. Imagine the universe as an infinitely large apartment building, with a different reality taking place in each apartment. Your awareness might currently reside in reality 2B, where you rent energy from the Creator. If you choose to repeatedly focus that energy on predicted annihilation, you and your apartment will likely be destroyed by fires, floods, explosions, tornadoes, or plagues.

If, however, you decide that you love your life, warts and all, and want it and the life forms in it to continue living and evolving, you can direct energy into creating well-being in your reality. Any portion of annihilation energy remaining in your awareness will manifest somewhere, and you could feel some effects because what takes place in other realities affects life in yours. If apartment 1R is gutted by fire, you might suffer smoke damage, a water main break that floods 4Y could leak into your reality, or a power outage on level three could cast you into darkness for a time. You experience some loss, but not annihilation.

Where do you live? Check your reality choices. Pay your rent to the Creator by respecting the energy of all life with loving thoughts and deeds.

REFLECTING ON YOU

Our bodies are composed of quadrillions of molecules that are in constant, rapid motion. All this activity generates an electromagnetic field around us. Unfortunately, our physical eyes cannot see the light waves of this energy field because their wavelengths do not fall within the visible spectrum.

Fortunately, our intuitive eyes can see the electromagnetic field just fine. This energy that emanates from our bodies—and from the bodies of animals, plants, and rocks—is known as an aura. The golden halo around the heads and bodies of angels and spiritual masters in paintings, is how the aura looks around people whose energy is harmonious, high, and devoted to loving the Creator.

To see your aura, stand in front of a full length mirror, with enough light to see your reflection, but without causing glare. It helps to hang a plain dark blanket or sheet on a wall behind you, so the background is uniform and dark. Close your eyes and breathe deeply into the bottom of your belly a few times. Center your awareness in your solar plexus. Open your eyes and look slightly to the right of your image, but without focusing. You will see yourself peripherally through your left eye, which is connected to your right brain, which sees intuitively and wholly. Then imagine you are seeing your whole being through your solar plexus. Keeping your eyes relaxed, you will see patches and swirls of colors around different areas of your body. They might range from golden white to black. Dull muddy colors usually indicate negative or compromised energy. Where they appear—head, heart, stomach, and so forth—tells you which activities you need to upgrade. Bright clear colors reflect healthy, free-flowing energy. The higher the quality of the energy you generate, the better shape you and your aura are in.

CREATIVE FREEDOM

IF you are suffering from the ho-hum humdrum of life, mired in routine, trapped by have-to-get-it-dones, your mind and spirit need a vacation. At least once a week do something purely creative. If you can be creative every day, if only for five minutes, you will enliven your psyche even more.

Webster's Dictionary defines the verb "create" as: "1: to bring into existence 2: to invest with a new form 3: to cause 4: to produce through imaginative skill." This is the essence of power, to connect with the energy of your vision and bring it into being by taking action. When you are being creative you shift into the imaginative realm of your right mind, yet use the analytical skills of your left brain, generating synergistic mental energy. The intensity of your involvement in the process makes you feel fully alive. When you create you are doing what the Creator does, which moves you into closer spiritual harmony.

Avoid being competitively creative. If you judge what you create as being better or worse than what somebody else has produced, you give the power of creation to your negative ego instead of your spirit. Simply enjoy the satisfaction of the experience itself. Take a photograph of a light-filled child, arrange flowers artfully, sketch a house or a co-worker, craft a form out of a lump of clay; make music, paste pictures and words together to make a collage, combine your clothes differently, write a poem, plant a seed, send an imaginative e-mail.

Opportunities to be creative abound. See each day as full of potential for creative expression, because you are bringing into being activities and experiences that did not previously exist. When your days are creative, your whole life becomes creative, and you are alive, powerful, and free.

HUMBLE-IZING

EVERYTHING in the universe affects everything else because everything is part of the same whole and so is connected. This we-are-all-one stuff rubs your negative self totally the wrong way. Your negative self wants to be master of the universe, not part of it. To this end, it steals your power and that of others, and separates you from sources of power: yourself, love, earth, spirit, the universe.

There is a simple act that takes your power away from your negative ego and returns it to you, reconnecting you with your loving, spiritual being. It comes from the Christian tradition, when Jesus Christ washed the feet of his disciples before giving them the commandment to "Love one another, as I have loved you." The ritual is now celebrated on Maundy Thursday, "maundy" deriving from the Latin *mandatum*, to command or mandate, but it can be performed by anyone, anytime, regardless of their religious or spiritual affiliations.

Ask a loved one to sit in a chair. Place a bowl on the floor and fill it with warm water. Add aromatic oil if you want to. Have a clean towel on hand. Your loved one places their feet in the water, and you humbly kneel on the floor before them. As you rub their feet, and sluice water over them, hold in your mind and heart the spirit of being there to serve them, helping them to let the light and love of the Creator flow through them to illuminate and empower their purpose on Earth. Tenderly dry the person's feet, and thank them for the privilege of serving them. Parents who are already washing the feet of their young children remind yourself as you do it that you are there to serve them in their growth.

Being a true master of your universe means having the power to control others, but choosing instead to use that power to serve them.

BODOMETER

Every day you are faced with hundreds of decisions. They can range from what purchases to make, to which strategy to use in business. Wouldn't it be marvelous to have a portable device you could use wherever you happened to be, that would accurately indicate the best course of action. Guess what? You already have such a device. Your intuition. It is given to you as part of the package of your life, and it comes in a handy carrying case—your body.

Even if you haven't listened to it much, your intuition is alive and well and just waiting to be heard. What it has to say is of great value because it operates outside the box of your conscious mind and so has access to a vaster realm of data. One of the instruments through which it can transmit information is your body. When you have a decision to make, make your best choice, but before taking action, take time to listen to what your body is saying. As you think about your decision, notice if your body feels tight, heavy, or tired. Does your stomach feel queasy, or as if a large lead weight were lodged in it? Do your heart and solar plexus feel closed, cold, dark? Such contrary physical feelings are your intuition's way of telling you it is probably not a choice that will further you.

When the choice you make is positive for you, your intuition will telegraph that information by making your body feel relaxed, buoyant, and energized. Your stomach will feel warm and calm, and your heart will feel open and light.

These same positive and negative physical responses can also indicate the truth or untruth of what other people say. Your body is a barometer that registers whether the intuitive forecast is cloudy or sunny. The final choice is always yours, but it certainly pays to take time to read the meter.

FREE HELP

Helping someone who is experiencing difficulties is a good, even noble, act, but before taking a step, examine your motivation. If you want to help because it makes you feel superior or praiseworthy, beware your negative ego, which operates by setting you up then knocking you down. If you are drawn to help because you need to be needed, that emptiness within you cannot be filled externally. If you have hidden expectations, and help so you can manipulate the person, you do yourself and the person a grave disservice. Initiating actions that are unbalanced tends to produce more imbalance.

The person in distress is usually in a victim mode. If you gallop in on your white charger—regardless of what gender you are—you automatically become the rescuer. It seems to be the role that is called for, but there is a third, as yet unrevealed, role waiting in the wings. Energy seeks balance through change. The person you helped will tire of being a victim and will seek balance by becoming the persecutor, making you the victim. The original helpee then takes on the role of rescuer. You will rail against being the victim and become the persecutor, casting the other person in their original role of victim. It is possible to shift roles in the triangle within minutes, or it can take months, even years.

The solution is to get off the ego stage and play a higher, heartier role. Remind yourself that you are on the planet to express the love and light of the Creator, especially to those who are in the dark and have lost touch with love. Realize that whatever resources you have to give, come to you by the grace of the Creator. When you gladly accept your spiritual role, you liberate all your actions. Then, unfettered by ego, needs, or expectations, you can give help freely.

ANGEL AT WORK

FOR centuries, major religions have recorded the intercessions of angels. Gothic and Renaissance artists painted angels, they appear throughout literature and history, and there is evidence of their influence in modern times.

Can so many people be wrong? There is a good chance they are onto something good, and you can be, too. Everyone has a guardian angel who watches over them, guiding, comforting, teaching, and protecting them. That means you have a guardian angel even if you do not believe you do. People didn't used to believe in ultraviolet light, but that didn't stop it from existing.

To connect with your guardian angel, begin by connecting with your breath. Sitting quietly, following your breathing, attunes you to your true self, the life-force, and the Creator, raising your vibration to be more attuned to your angel's. Ask your angel to help you open to it and its messages. Asking is key because your angel, respecting your free will, waits to be invited into your life. Write your angel a letter asking for the help and guidance you seek.

Angelic energy has no gender, but your guardian angel could show you a mental image of itself in male or female form, with or without wings and halo. Your angel is usually so delighted you want to talk with it that it makes its presence known to you immediately. You may experience a profound feeling of peace and joy. In some instances, you may even smell an aroma of roses or some other sweet fragrance. Or you may feel a tingling sensation. Be alert for events of serendipity and synchronicity that herald, "Angel at work!"

You are an angel in training; any step you take toward love and light, wisdom and compassion, your guardian angel is there to support and nurture.

THE ART OF QUESTIONS

THE art of asking questions is shaped by what you want to know and colored by why you want to know it. When you want to know more about a person because you are interested in them, you make them feel special and build strong lines of communication. When you inquire about someone's needs because you want to help, you make the person feel cared for and add depth. When you request information about a problem to help bring about a solution, you make the person feel supported and create symmetry.

These are three of the primary motivations that make asking questions artful. Other motivations turn questions insidious instead of ingenious. Asking questions to keep the focus off you because you are unwilling to reveal yourself, lacks balance. Interrogating someone as a power play to put them on the spot, lacks harmony. Possibly the worst motivation is to ask penetrating questions about someone's private business or personal affairs so you can use the information against them or turn it to your advantage. This not only lacks integrity, but the negative energy you set in motion will rub off on you. None of these motivations are constructive, so they are not powerful.

Questions that *are* powerful are the basics. Ask someone how they are and really mean it. Listen to their answer not only with your ears, but with your heart and intuition. Acknowledge their response by commenting on it, then use it as a springboard to ask another question. You might want to know more about what they said, or better understand it. Ask about their interests.

Conversation begins as a blank canvas. Questions are the brushes, and words the paint that create form and color. Create conversational works of art!

TRUE TRUTH

THERE is truth and then there is *truth*. The first kind is something that appears to be true on the surface, or maybe you want it to be true, but it isn't true all the way through. It's a secondary truth. A primary *truth* is as true deep down as it is on the surface. It is consistently true. Want to tell the difference?

Think of a simple sentence that describes how you feel about yourself, your work, your life, or another person. For example: I am happy. I love myself. My work is fulfilling. I am in charge of my life. I respect so-and-so.

Say the sentence aloud, as if you were saying it in conversation with another person. What facial, hand, foot, or body movements do you make when you say the sentence? Do you raise an eyebrow, curl your toes, drum your fingers, tighten your jaw, swing your foot, or shrug your shoulders?

Physical gestures such as these occur when your subconscious mind knows that the statement you made is only partially true, or maybe even not true at all. You unconsciously use such gestures to try to convince yourself and others that what you are saying is tried and true, but they are actually flags that signal untruth. The more movements you make, the less true the statement. A primary truth stands strong and balanced on it's own two feet; it does not need gestures to support it.

Try out different sentences until you find words that flow from the depths of your heart, as water flows from a deep spring. When you speak your truth you will feel a sense of calm, clarity, and power. This is how you, as well as others, can recognize your true truth.

AYE, EYE

THE eyes have it. They are the part of our bodies most closely connected to our brains, and they can even be considered extensions of the brain. They are our windows to the world through which we are able to see out, and light and information can pass in. The brain processes approximately three billion bytes of information a second, and two billion of them are received through the eyes.

Your eyes need and deserve the best care you can give them, especially in this age of information when you are probably using your eyes even more, and for longer periods of time at a stretch. In addition to having them examined once a year by a qualified optometrist, there are simple, helpful measures you can take. One way to stretch your eyes is to vary the distances on which you focus. If you spend hours looking at a computer screen, or columns of figures, periodically look out a window at the horizon. If you spend hours looking at distant objects, take breaks to read a magazine or look at your feet.

Shutting your eyes tightly for three seconds squeezes the old blood out. When you open them, freshly oxygenated blood rushes in, bringing new life to tired eyes. Blinking your eyes rapidly will also refresh them. Moving your eyes in circles—up, left, down, right, up—helps strengthen them.

To both soothe and energize your eyes, briskly rub the palms of your hands together, then gently place the heel of each palm over your closed eyes. The friction caused by rubbing your hands together sparks energy in your palms, and that energy is transferred to your eyes when you cover them. Hold the heels of your palms against your eyes until you feel the energy ebb, then repeat.

When you see to the care of your eyes, they will see better for you.

COULD IS GOOD

I should shine my shoes. I should lose weight. I should be nicer to Stan at the office. I should wash the car. I should be more supportive of Lucy. I should call my parents. I should not drive so fast. I should read more.

You should try harder. You should stop smoking. You should listen to what I say. You should see the show at the Whitney. You should pay attention to your dreams. You should stop using the word "should."

How many times a day do you tell yourself or someone else that you, or they should or should not do something? Can you feel an inner part of you wince? Does some part of your body tense? Saying or hearing the word "should" immediately plugs you into an authority energy that is often associated on a subconscious level with someone who made you feel uncomfortable. "Should" might remind you of an overbearing parent, a strict teacher, or a demanding boss. The word "should" means obligation, feels restrictive, and brings on the pressure of fearing you won't meet the expectation. Is it any wonder that you feel resistant to doing something when there is a "should" in front of it?

The antidote is to pay close attention to what you say, and every time you hear yourself say "should," replace it with "could." Where "should" negates your free will, "could" offers the power of choice and grants freedom. Where "should" is closed, "could" is open. Where "should" imposes limitation, "could" presents possibilities. When someone says you should do something, substitute "could." I could wash the car, or I could call my parents, or I could drive slower. The choice is mine. You could try harder, or you could see the show at the Whitney, or you could use the word "could." The freedom of choice is yours.

INTUITIVE MUSCLE

Everyone has a subconscious mind, and all our subconscious minds are connected. Being consciously aware of the information they share is known as intuition. The problem is that the emphasis on industry and technology in the last three hundred years has led us to be skeptical of intuition, and consequently we don't use it as often as we could. Like a muscle that isn't used, our intuition has become weak.

To strengthen your intuition it helps to exercise it on a regular basis. The only workout garb you need is a positive attitude. Be open to the possibility that you can be intuitive, just as when you were young you were open to the possibility that you could be a singer, a sailor, a runner, or good at math.

Daily life offers many opportunities to exercise your intuitive muscle:

- When the phone rings, take a deep breath before answering and mentally ask your subconscious who is calling, allowing an image or a name to pop into your conscious mind.
- Boiling an egg? Don't use a timer. Instead let your subconscious extend itself through the shell to tell you when it is done just the way you like it.
- When you are talking with someone, remind yourself to listen to them at a deeper level than hearing their words. What sense impressions do you receive about how the person is really feeling and how honest they are being?
- When your computer or car develops a glitch, ask your subconscious to scan the innards of the machine and tell you where the problem lies.
- When your body develops a glitch, ask your subconscious to scan it, and tell you what is causing the problem.

Exercise your intuition often and make it strong.

SAFETY LIGHT

WHENEVER you get in a vehicle to go somewhere, you greatly increase your chances of arriving safely at your destination by mentally picturing the vehicle being filled and surrounded with light. It works whether you are operating the vehicle, or someone else is in charge of it. The vehicle can be a car, plane, train, bus, truck, boat, subway, tram, tractor, or canoe.

As soon as you enter the conveyance, take a moment to be aware of its physical structure and space so you can picture it in your mind with your eyes closed. As you see or sense the image mentally, visualize bright white light filling it and surrounding it. See the light filling every nook and cranny, and anyone else who is present. Make sure the bubble of light surrounding the vehicle is whole. As you picture the light, say, "The light fills and surrounds this _____, keeping it, its occupants, its contents, its activities, and everyone and everything around it completely safe, in all ways at all times." Visualize yourself and the vehicle arriving safely and on time at your destination.

Images are the native language of your subconscious mind, so it gets the picture. Your subconscious then helps what you have visualized become a physical reality, because that's its job. Keep in mind that your subconscious is literal, so choose your words carefully, because you will get what you ask for. For example, if you say, "The light fills and surrounds this _____, so that no *harm* comes to it, etc.," your subconscious hears the word "harm," but doesn't compute the word no, and now has the impression that you in fact want harm to be inflicted. Always state the positive.

Traveling with the light is the ticket to being safe.

SOUND SENSE

Y ou have undoubtedly noticed how some sounds promote harmony with your peaceful, powerful self, and others create such static and interference that you feel beside yourself with agitation and annoyance. This is because sound waves directly affect your brain waves, which affect your thinking, which in turn affects your actions, emotions, and physical health.

Sound travels in waves though solids, liquids, and gases, and the waves cause molecules to compress and expand as they pass. Imagine how they affect your brain. In fact, sound travels faster through water than air, and your brain is seventy percent water. How soft or loud sound is can either soothe or stress, with sound becoming noise when wave vibrations are irregular, or several unrelated vibrations occur simultaneously. Avoid noise because its dissonance creates discord within you by confusing your thinking and jangling your energy.

Listen to sounds whose waves cleanse your mind, smooth your feelings, refresh your energy, and make your spirit float. It is now recommended that infants listen to classical music every day because it stimulates their brain neurons. It also has a positive effect on adult brains, and the sixty beats per minute help stabilize your heart rate. Some jazz, blues, New Age, and mellow pop music can lower blood pressure and diminish pain. Bells, Tibetan finger symbols, crystal bowls, tuning forks, harps, and violin strings, which produce sustained tones, fine tune your energy on every level. Generally, higher frequency sounds raise lower frequency energy. You can also hang chimes inside or outside your home to delight your ears, your mind, and your heart.

It makes sound sense to respect your sense of sound.

IT'S A DRAW

ARE your better self and not-so-good self having a showdown? Does your good self win one day, and then your ornery self gains the upper hand the next? Here's a way to give the winning advantage to your better self.

Draw a picture of you behaving in a way that does not further you. Maybe eating or drinking something that isn't healthy. Or yelling at someone. Or being a couch potato. Or doing something that endangers yourself or others.

You don't have to be Rembrandt to do this effectively. Drawing cartoon stick figures and outlines of objects works just fine. Draw a circle for your head, sketching in your expression when you're engaged in this unhealthy habit. Also draw the clothes you wear and color them in. When it's done, use a thick black crayon or marker to draw an X through the drawing, from corner to corner. Write NO! across the center of the drawing. Tear or cut the paper into small pieces and burn them, flush them, bury them in the earth, or throw them to the wind.

Using only brightly colored crayons or markers, draw a picture of you being healthy, happy, peaceful, prosperous, and powerful. Draw your clothes and your expression. In your favorite bright color, or in gold or silver, write YES!! at the top of the page. At the bottom of the page sign your name just the way you do on checks or letters, with that day's date. Post the picture where you will see it often, on a wall, or inside the door of your closet or medicine cabinet.

Your hand has a strong connection to your brain, so what you draw becomes powerfully imprinted in your consciousness. Signing a drawing claims ownership of it. Dating it activates the energy. You win the draw!

ENERGY SHIELD

Your physical body is a powerhouse of vibrating molecules, which create a bubble of energy around you. The electromagnetic field is shaped like an egg, being narrower around your head, then widening down from there. Depending on how spiritually alive you are, it can extend out from your body anywhere from a few inches to several yards, or even more. The aura of the Lord Gautama Buddha was reputed to extend two hundred miles.

It is a good idea to check your energy egg on a regular basis. You can do this by looking at it intuitively. First breathe slowly and deeply several times to calm and center yourself. By keeping your conscious mind focused on your breathing you open the door to your subconscious mind, which can see your energy. Mentally ask your subconscious to show you a mental image of the energy surrounding you. Focus on your breathing and keep your mind open.

A picture of you surrounded by an egg-shaped energy field will pop into your mind. You might even sense the energy around you as well as see it. Examine your energy egg carefully, checking for cracks in the outer shell, weak areas, holes, and dimness. The shell of energy is like a shield. If the shield is not whole and strong and bright, your energy can leak out, just as raw egg leaks out through a cracked shell. If the shell of energy is not intact, you also become vulnerable to intrusions by the negative energy and thoughtforms of other people and low-level spirits, which can drain you or block the flow of your energy. Visualize the egg of light being bright and full.

The high or low energy of everything you think, feel, see, say, hear, touch, eat, and do, affects the health of your energy. Choose positive, high-energy actions in all areas to repair and strengthen your shield.

DAILY DEEDS

In today's hectic world we have so much to do each day, but seemingly not enough time in which to do it. Because of this pressure, we tend to focus on what we have not done, instead of giving ourselves credit for what we *have* done. Emphasizing the negative reinforces a feeling of being inadequate, an attitude that can all too quickly become a self-fulfilling prophecy. This imbalance in your self-esteem can also exhaust your mental and physical energy.

Whether you are engaged in commercial business, or in the business of managing a family, it will enhance both your self-esteem and your energy to acknowledge your accomplishments. At the end of each day, jot down what you accomplished in a "Daily Deeds" notebook. Be sure to enter *every* deed, from the mundane to the magnificent. Write down that you saved the company from losing an account, and also note that you changed a burned out light bulb.

Another way of keeping track of your accomplishments is to make a "Things to Do" list in the morning. Making such a list helps thwart procrastination and gives you an objective overview of your day that helps curb any tendency to set unrealistic goals. Check off each entry after you have done it. Be sure to add anything you do that was not on the list.

When you see in writing all that you have done, you will more easily realize what a capable and valuable person you are. You will also be kinder to yourself about tasks you did not complete, because you'll see that you have done the best you could.

Giving yourself credit for your daily deeds boosts self-esteem, restores balance, eases tension, and gives you more energy to do what you need to do.

THANKS FOR THE FUTURE

IF you're human, there is a good chance that there is something you want that you don't currently have. Maybe there's a special town you want to move to, or a promotion you're hankering after. Maybe you want to be more fit, or you are saving for a new computer, car, or house. Maybe you want to be more peaceful.

One way to help your goal become a reality is to give heartfelt thanks for the success of it now, as if it has already occurred. The reason this works is that it is only your left-brain conscious mind that perceives time as taking place sequentially, with the past, present, and future following one another in a straight line. Your more right-brain subconscious mind steps off the time line and away from it, seeing the past, present, and future at the same time. It also perceives your mental images as being real, and bases your physical reality on them.

This means that when you create a vivid mental image of you achieving your goal, even though it appears in the future to your conscious mind, to your subconscious it is happening here and now. When you energize the mental image of success with positive emotions, your subconscious immediately begins orchestrating everything needed for the mental image to become physical.

One of the highest energy and most powerful positive emotions is gratitude. Mentally picture yourself having accomplished your goal, then feel how glad you are to have succeeded. Giving thanks for your future becomes especially potent if you are a heart patient or cancer survivor.

Say thank you, verbally and emotionally, for the success of every goal you have. Really put your heart into it. Thank your Creator, the universe, your guardian angel, your guides, power animals. Thank yourself. The future is now.

BODY MAINTENANCE

Some people take better care of their cars than they do their bodies, lavishing care, even affection, on them. But how far would you get without your body? Where would you be? Maybe you'd exist somewhere in time and space, but certainly not here in this physical reality.

It might seem to be stating the obvious to say that your body is essential to your well-being, but people tend to forget that they have just the one. They neglect it or abuse it. They take it for granted. They don't give it the respect it deserves for its tireless service.

The body has been referred to as the temple of the soul. That may sound too grand for your taste, nonetheless it *is* a vehicle for your mind and spirit. Unlike a car, however, you can't trade it in for a new model. At least not in this lifetime.

Like a car, your body will run better and for longer if you keep it filled with high octane gas, keep the oil clean, check for wear, and perform scheduled maintenance checkups.

How long has it been since you took your body in for a complete physical exam? Chances are your car has been in for a tune-up more recently than your body. Make an appointment to see your doctor as soon as possible and take your body into the body shop for a tune-up. Have a complete physical exam: blood pressure, weight, blood tests, urine analysis, cholesterol, EKG, reflexes, muscle strength, fat percentage, liver, gallbladder, thyroid, and so forth.

A strong and healthy body gets better mileage. It also provides a more comfortable ride for your mind and spirit.

UNIVERSAL RELATIONS

How would you describe your relationship with your mother? Did she love you unconditionally? Was she emotionally supportive of your emotions? Or did she withhold love? Was she critical? How was your relationship with your father? Did he express his love? Did he take an interest in your interests? Or was he emotionally remote? Did you have to earn his respect?

How would you describe your relationship with the Creator? The chances are good that it is similar to your relationships with your mother and father, because it is a natural inclination to project the qualities of your parents onto the Creator. If your parents were loving, supportive, and generous, you will expect the universe to be the same. If they were unloving, critical, and stingy, you will expect the universe to treat you the same way.

Seeing the Creator as your parents limits the amount of love and support you receive from the universe. This is not because the universe is punishing you, but because your limited view has created only a narrow opening through which love can flow. It's a little like putting a box over your head and squinting at the sky through a pinhole— your field of vision is cramped and not much light flows in.

Cast off the parental box. Open your mind and heart to the reality that the Creator loves you far beyond any love you can fathom. There is not a second in your life when you are required to prove yourself worthy. The Creator loves you *all* the time and *never* withholds love. You might separate yourself from the Creator, but It never separates Itself from you. Whenever you earnestly ask for forgiveness, the Creator embraces you with love and healing. Know that the Creator cares about every breath you take, and holds you joyfully in Its heart.

KNOCK IT

You have probably heard the expression, "Don't knock it," referring to not disparaging something. Usually you don't want to knock your head either, because it could disparage your brain, but here's an exception.

Go right ahead and knock your noggin—but gently! Begin by using just the pads of your fingertips, tapping lightly all over your head with both hands. Don't tap your face, but do tap everywhere else: the top of your forehead, the crown of your head, the sides, the upper back, and the lower back near your neck. Do not tap so hard it hurts; find the amount of pressure that is comfortable for you. You can tap both hands in unison, or alternate the rhythm. Experiment with pressure and rhythm to see what feels best. If using the pads of your fingertips feels comfortable, then try using your knuckles.

As you tap or rap your head, you will notice that certain areas begin to tingle or feel warm. Body reflexologists say that tapping the energy points on your head stimulates energy centers throughout your body, possibly improving digestion, urinary function, and sexual energy.

The tapping also seems to increase blood circulation to the scalp, helping to make your scalp healthy, which may help your hair grow and be more healthy. Tapping your skull might also increase blood flow to your brain. It definitely seems to wake it up and make it more alert. It could also cause your brain to release endorphin hormones, which increase your feeling of well-being.

Knocking some sense into your head can be sensational. Don't knock knocking it until you try it.

HAVING DIRECTION

IN living our busy, individual lives we tend to forget that we are part of a much larger whole. We live in a world that extends well beyond the boundaries of our bodies, homes, cities, states, countries, continents, planet, solar system, and galaxy. We are part of humankind, nature, and the cosmos.

To reinforce those connections, Native Americans honor the four directions in their Medicine Wheel rituals. The Medicine Wheel is a mirror of the universe, both seen and unseen, with all parts connected to all other parts.

Each direction has its own special meaning and energy. The east is connected to beginnings, rebirth, and illumination. It is represented by the eagle who has clarity of sight and sees far. The color of the east is yellow gold.

The south is connected to growth, trust, and the heart. It is represented by the mouse who lives close to the ground. The color is green.

The west is connected to introspection and change. It is represented by the bear who hibernates. The color is black.

The north is the place of the mind, of wisdom and power. It is represented by the strong, far roaming buffalo. The color is white.

Connect with the power of the four directions by facing the east, then turn sunward to the south, west, and north, greeting each direction. Every experience you have relates to one of the directions; meditate on your situation facing that direction. To call the energy of a direction to you, wear the corresponding color, or carry a picture of the animal that represents the direction.

Honoring the four directions gives you direction for the day and for your life.

QUOTATION QUOTIENT

FROM ancient to modern times, thousands of famous creative, intelligent, wise, innovative, witty, and perspicacious people have lived, and fortunately for us have talked and written, or had their words written down. Their singular and discerning perspectives on life are shared with us as quotations.

A single astute quotation can throw open a window through which we can gaze upon new, intriguing vistas of thought and understanding. Or it might cast light on a facet of an idea we have not considered before. It can also strengthen our own beliefs and experiences by confirming them in a succinct, original manner. A finely turned quotation can touch our hearts, uplift our energy, move us to action, raise our goals. It can make us smile.

If a single quotation can do all this, imagine what several might achieve. As you read books, glance through magazines, watch television, listen to the radio, or browse through a book of quotations, jot down any quote that speaks to you either through its wit or wisdom. Keep a journal of positive quotations.

Periodically read through your journal, choosing two or three quotations that have special meaning for your current circumstances. Write or type each one on a separate piece of paper, index card, or adhesive backed label. Use different colored inks and papers so they are more eye-catching, then post them where you will be sure to see them each day, at home, in your car, and at work.

Every time you read an inspiring quotation its message becomes part of you. Raising your quotation quotient raises the amount of positive information stored in your subconscious, and raises your energy, maybe even your IQ.

ORANGE FLUSH

WOULDN'T it be nifty if your clothes never became soiled and you never had to wash them? Unfortunately, they do and you do. Just as your body, clothes, house, and car become dirty and need to be cleaned, so does your energy.

Every person's body is composed of molecules in motion, which generate energy. As you go about your daily life, you are exposed to the psychic grime of others. Your own fears, pains, angers, jealousies, stress, and negative thoughts also contribute to ugly toxic build-up. Just as a dirty body is unsanitary and can eventually make you sick, so can soiled energy. Fortunately there is an easy, powerful, one-shot cleaning method available at your nearest imagination on the love-of-self shelf.

Mentally picture yourself sitting or standing in the center of a large, clear Plexiglas bubble. At the top of it, over your head, is a faucet. At the bottom of the bubble, under your feet, is a drain with the stopper in place.

Turn on the faucet above your head. Liquid orange light, in a bright, beautiful shade, begins to flow over you down to your feet. As the bubble fills, the orange light flows both around you and through you. The orange light dissolves negative energy, tension, and toxins, both physical and nonphysical.

When the bubble is full, sit in the orange light until you sense that it has done its job. Then pull the stopper on the drain. As you watch the liquid orange light drain out, you notice that it has turned the color of muddy bath water because of all the dirty energy it has broken down and flushed out. You and your energy are now sparkling clean and healthy.

PENDULUMS SWING

THE dimension of your mind known as the subconscious has access to information that your limited conscious mind does not. Your subconscious has a difficult time getting its information through to you, because your rational conscious mind analyzes the information and blocks it as being illogical.

A device that helps your subconscious express its knowledge directly is a pendulum. You can make one quickly by slipping a ring from your finger and onto a thin chain necklace, or tie a piece of string or fishing line around it. For a more balanced weight, use a cone-shaped wooden or metal bob, or a crystal, with the point down. The length of string or chain is usually somewhere between five and ten inches. Try different lengths to see what feels comfortable.

To determine how your subconscious is going to indicate yes and no answers, draw a circle on a piece of paper. Sitting with your feet flat on the floor, hold the string of the pendulum between your thumb and index finger, the weight over the center of the circle. Ask a question to which the answer is yes. "Is my name_____?" The pendulum might swing left to right, top to bottom, clockwise, or counterclockwise. How it swings will be yes. Ask two more yes answer questions, mentally reaffirming that this is yes. Then ask a question to which the answer is no. "Am I nine feet tall?" Note the direction of the swing. Ask two more no questions, reaffirming the direction of no.

Now you can ask your subconscious questions about your life. Hold it over food, vitamins, and medicine, asking, "Is this healthy for me?" In a room in your home or office ask if negative energy is present. Ask what actions further you. Combine the information with what you know consciously to arrive at the best action to take.

MAKING PEACE

IT is usually a difficult and sad part of life when people you know die. The difficulty and sadness are compounded when you wish the person was there to talk with, or you want to ask them for forgiveness, or perhaps offer forgiveness.

Although you cannot talk with the person in the flesh, it is possible to talk with him or her in spirit. Many people believe that death occurs physically, but not spiritually. Imagine that you are sitting across from the person in a place that was special to the two of you. It might be a particular room in a house, a table at a restaurant, or a spot outdoors in nature. See and sense the place, then see and sense the person being with you. If tears come, let them.

Tell the person everything you have been wanting to say to them. Tell them you miss them. Or maybe you are angry they left you, even if it doesn't seem right to be angry with someone for dying. (Many people feel angry and are too embarrassed to admit it.) Tell them how you are doing. If there are things you wish you had done or not done, said or not said, talk about them. Ask the person to forgive you. Often you will feel flooded with love that washes away those regrets. If the person hurt you, offer forgiveness when you are ready.

Sometimes you will receive a strong impression of the person responding to what you are saying. You may even hear certain phrases, or specific information in your mind. Let your heart gauge the authenticity of it.

Expressing love and resolving conflicts in this way, helps release both your spirit and theirs. You become free to fully lead your life on earth, and the spirit of the person who has died is freed from the energy of the earth to lead their life on the spiritual planes. This is a truly lovely gift to yourself and the person's spirit.

ENERGY CENTERS

IF you are looking for some power to plug into, you have seven outlets right in your body. These energy centers are referred to in ancient Sanskrit manuscripts of the Hindus as *chakras*, a word that means wheels of fire, because the energy radiates out from each center and spins in a circular pattern. The chakra centers serve as links between the physical world and spiritual energy and awareness. Each of the seven chakras is located near one of your endocrine glands, and is associated with a specific color and note of the seven-toned musical scale, as well as particular mental, emotional, or spiritual states.

1. *Root chakra*: Gonads, base of spine; red; low C. Pulls magnetic energy up from the Earth that primarily affects physical vitality.
2. *Second chakra*: Spleen, left of spine near spleen; orange; D. Receives electromagnetic energy from the sun and affects emotional balance.
3. *Third chakra*: Adrenals, solar plexus; yellow; E. Receives energy from the sun, and is linked to the intellect and subconscious.
4. *Fourth chakra*: Thymus, heart; green; F. Flows in horizontally, linking you to supraconscious, and inspires compassion.
5. *Fifth chakra*: Thyroid, throat; blue; G. Electric and flows down from above. Considered gateway to spiritual awareness.
6. *Sixth chakra*: Pituitary, center of head above brows; indigo; A. Its energy affects your spiritual inspiration and intuition.
7. *Seventh chakra*: Pineal, crown of head; Violet; B. The door to the Divine.

You can raise the energy of the kundalini serpent that lies sleeping at the base of your spine by the use of breathing, colors, mental imagery, and sound. Inhaling deeply draws in the life energy of the sun. You can also visualize the color of a particular chakra flowing around you and breathe it in to stimulate that chakra, or play the corresponding note. You are energy. Plug in.

HARMONY AT HOME

Did you know that the height at which you hang a mirror can be hazardous to your health?

According to the ancient Chinese art of feng shui, the placement of everything in your home and office affects your energy. The Chinese believe that universal life energy, *chi*, flows through everything and everyone. A building is viewed as a body, and so is each room. Doors are mouths and windows are eyes. Halls are like veins through which the life blood, chi, flows.

For harmony and health to exist, chi must be able to flow freely. If it is blocked by doors, furniture, beams, or corners, health and harmony are compromised. The effects are similar to having the flow of your blood impeded. The surrounding region becomes stressed, and other areas suffer because life-giving blood is not reaching them. The object is to restore the flow of chi.

Hang mirrors at head height. If they are too low, they lower chi and can cause the inhabitants of the house to suffer headaches. The larger a mirror, the greater the benefits it bestows. Position a mirror to draw scenes from nature into a room. Reflections of plants and water can increase the flow of money.

Plants symbolize life and growth, and increase energy. The more lush they are, the better. Large healthy plants by your front door attract good chi.

Lights and lamps are symbolic of the sun and energize chi.

Arrange the furniture in your living room so it faces the living room door. People sitting in it will feel more relaxed and secure. In your office, position your desk so you view the door.

Free flowing chi helps physical, mental, emotional, and spiritual harmony.

CHARMED

THE practice of carrying a good luck charm may date back to prehistoric cave dwellers. Virtually every culture since then has used amulets for protection against harm, and talismans for attracting blessings and good fortune. A charm is usually fashioned out of wood, metal, shell, or bone, in the image of a holy person or god, a spiritual symbol, or an animal. The amulet or talisman can be worn as jewelry, carried in a pocket, or hung in the home.

Both amulets and talismans are designed to empower their owner. The premise is that the image of a powerful person, symbol, or animal connects you to the energy of their spirits. You can also call forth the power of the charm to help you. When you look at the image, you are reminded of your connection, further strengthening the bond. Amulets are made to be seen not only by the wearer, but by mean-spirited spirits who might wish to cause harm. When they see the sacred power with which you are aligned, they leave you alone.

Choose an amulet or talisman whose powers you believe in. The image can depict someone who is a religious inspiration, or a spiritual teacher. It can be a symbol such as a star, the Egyptian ankh (which symbolizes life), the Christian cross, or the Sufis' winged heart. Carry a small carving of one of your power animals. In France a golden angel pendant is given to newborns as a symbol of the angel which watches over them, but you never grow too old to keep an angel with you. In many areas of the world the serpent is considered a powerful protector and source of energy. Put a Jewish mezuzah on your door. Wear a crescent moon or a butterfly.

Whichever amulet or talisman you choose, your life is sure to be charmed.

THE MATTER WITH MATTER

LIFE on earth seems so real, doesn't it? So solid, so immovable, so big, so gosh darn physical. Metaphysicists, shamans, and Eastern spiritual leaders, however, say it's all done with smoke and mirrors, that life on earth is an illusion, a dream. They look to the nonphysical states for their truths and power.

Why then are we so convinced physical life is real? A partial explanation is that most of us look at life through the lenses of our logical left brains, which are not suited to processing what cannot be defined, dissected, quantified, or circumscribed. Anything that falls outside its rational parameters, the left brain rejects.

We have also become removed from nature, and so from the Creator, and have lost touch with our imaginative, intuitive, infinite right brains. Beginning in the 1750s, the Industrial Revolution conditioned us to put our trust in concrete devices instead of spiritual forces, and now we put our faith in technology.

The problem with believing that matter is the only reality that matters, is that we give our power to it. We allow the seeming physical denseness of its presence to rule us, which is like a chef letting food do the cooking. The earth does indeed nourish us, but we have the power to be master chefs of our reality.

The next time the physical world is getting in your way, or getting you down, emphatically remind yourself that it is not as unyielding as it appears. Physicists have proved that matter is really light trapped by gravity, and Werner Heisenberg's uncertainty principle experiments showed that an observer affects how physical reality behaves. Do more than be an observer of your world; take charge of matters by focusing the energy of your thoughts, emotions, and actions to influence physical energy and cook up a delicious, nutritious reality.

DAYDREAMER

In school you were probably reprimanded for daydreaming, and certainly there are inappropriate, even unsafe times to indulge in daydreaming, but other than choosing your times well, do indulge! Daydreaming is relaxing because you are not exerting energy to control it. Freed of constraints, your imagination can come out and play, helping you be more creative. You might find yourself rehearsing future events, releasing unpleasant emotions from the past or fears about the future, or solving problems. In your daydreams you can be whomever you want, wherever you want. Your body can be standing in a line, but your mind can be on a beach in Tahiti. The daydreaming state also allows images to flow spontaneously from your subconscious and supraconscious selves to your conscious mind.

Daydreams are usually unfolding scenarios in which you figure prominently in the activity taking place. Because a daydream contains words, which come from the left hemisphere of your brain, and mental images, which spring from the right hemisphere, daydreams engage both the linear and the imaginative aspects of your mind. This helps the two sides work in harmony and stimulates mental energy, increasing your sense of well-being.

According to a study conducted by psychologist Jerome Singer at Yale University, 96 percent of people daydream, so the chances are excellent that you are already a daydreamer. It is also now thought that the purpose of sleep is not so much to rest your body as it is to rest your brain. Dreaming during the day gives your mind much needed breaks from the mental rigors of daily life. Wander through the infinitely varied landscape of your mind, and there is no telling what discoveries you might make. Be a daydreamer!

THERE'S NO COMPARISON

It is a common inclination to want to compare yourself to others. Is Jane better looking, smarter, richer, more popular, faster, stronger, more creative than I am? Am I better looking, smarter, richer, more popular, faster, stronger, more creative than Jane?

When you compare yourself to others, either you or the other person is bound to come up short. What at first appears to be a win/lose situation is really lose/lose, because it is not empowering for anyone. Here's why.

Personal comparisons are initiated not by your heart, but by your negative self, which is determined to prevent you from becoming truly powerful. This is its *raison d'etre*, because as long as you are powerless, or feel you are, it has a life. The instant you are powerful, your negative self is out of a job.

When you think you have won by being better, you are immediately caught in an illusion of feeling powerful. The feeling lacks authenticity because it doesn't originate from a constructive action and it doesn't enhance anyone's well-being. If you lose in the comparison, you're caught in the "depowerizing" syndrome of feeling less powerful, believing you're less than, then behaving less powerfully.

Any desire to measure yourself against another lures you into a trap. Outfox your negative ego by not making comparisons. You are unique in the world, with your own special combination of qualities and talents. Appreciate who you are and what you can do, without measuring yourself against others, who are also unique. It's not how much or how little you have, but what you do with it that counts. There is no comparison!

MAKE A STATEMENT

How do you get from where you are to where you're going? If you want to go out to eat, how do you accomplish it? Even before you transport yourself to a restaurant, the success of your efforts rests upon your purpose. If you do not know what you want to eat, you do not know where to go, and you can waste valuable time and energy going to undesirable restaurants, or wind up settling for less.

The metaphor holds true for anything you want to do in life, whether it's being more fit, closing a deal, or having a relationship. If you are vague about what you want, you can waste time and energy on unproductive actions, and often settle for less.

Such misdirected efforts can be avoided by being clear about what you want at the outset. First, formulate a mental statement that concisely captures your desire and intention. "I am able to lift/run/score _____ by (date)." "The terms of the deal that are acceptable are _____." "In a loving relationship I must have _____."

Then think about *why* you want to accomplish that particular goal. Knowing why you want to do something reveals more information about the what, and also activates emotional energy. The combination of knowing both what and why strengthens your determination more than either one by itself. Explore the whys beyond the obvious, being completely honest. "I want to be more fit to look more attractive and impress John."

Write a short paragraph, perhaps three or four sentences, describing your goal and why you want it. Sign it and date it. Hang it on a wall.

When you are clear about what you want and why, you will arrive at your destination more easily and efficiently, because your subconscious and supraconscious minds will also be clear about it and will help clear the way.

OPENING DOORS

Our free will is a gift from the Creator, who respects us so much that It gives us the freedom to make our own decisions, win, lose, or draw. It is in making choices that we grow, learning from both our mistakes and our accomplishments.

Having free will does not mean we have to go it alone. During the times when the gift feels more like a burden than a blessing, we can ask the Creator and our guardian angels for help. The operative word here is "ask." When you cannot find your way, ask for guidance. When the going is painful, ask for healing. When darkness descends, ask for light. When your responsibilities weigh you down, ask for strength. If you feel alone, ask for love to be present.

Maybe you think it sounds easy in theory, but know from experience how asking for help—from anyone—can make you feel exposed and vulnerable because you are admitting to a need. As the "asker," you feel as if you are handing the power for your well-being over to the "askee." These feelings are normal, but the truth is that the act of asking for help shows strength not weakness.

If you do not ask, you do not receive, or do not receive as much as you could. This is partly because the Creator and your guardian angel totally respect your free will decisions and your growth process. They intervene unasked mainly in emergencies when a choice you have made results in an event that does not further your growth. Otherwise they do not act until you ask them to. As soon as you do ask, they go into action to bring you what you need.

It does not matter how you envision your higher forces, or what you call them. Sincerely asking any loving higher force for help opens the door between the physical and the spiritual, allowing their help to flow to you more fully.

CLOTHED IN ENERGY

You might think that concern about what you wear is superficial and vain. You might think that caring about your clothes is irrelevant to what is important in life. You might even think that such concern would be fertile ground for your negative ego. You might think any of these thoughts, but you would be limiting yourself and your potential.

Everything in life is energy, and everything is connected. This means that clothes are energy, and they are closely connected to your energy. They are also an interface between you and other people's energy. The energy of the fabrics your clothes are made of vibrates at different frequencies. It is probably safe to say that natural fabrics that were at one time part of the earth, such as cotton, linen, wool, and silk, have higher energy than synthetic fabrics, although man-made materials certainly have their place. The colors of your clothes also vibrate at different rates. Clear bright colors tend to emit higher energy than muddy dark colors. Earth tones, however, are grounding.

Clothes do more than cover your nakedness and keep you warm or cool. The style and energy of your clothes affects your self-esteem and vice versa. When you feel good about yourself you choose clothes that flatter you. When you don't feel good about yourself you tend to throw on whatever is handy, and usually settle for whatever is handy in other areas of your life as well; relationships and jobs for example. Instead, when your self-esteem is frayed or torn, mend it by wearing your best and brightest apparel. Clothes are your self-image brought to the outside and made physical. They are fodder for your negative ego only if you compare your clothes to others' clothes.

Your clothes tailor your image and your image tailors your clothes. What image energy will you choose to wear today?

HIGHER HELP

WHEN you first arrive on the planet you are completely dependent on others for your physical survival. As you grow in strength and experience, you learn to do more and more for yourself. Your increasing self-sufficiency begins to threaten your negative ego, which believes that it can only be powerful if you aren't. In its wily way, your negative self tries to turn your eagerness for independence to its advantage. It tells you to do it all yourself, that you do not need help from anyone, including the Creator. It even leads you to believe that you will be a stronger person if you achieve your goals on your own, and your accomplishments will be more valuable. To keep you isolated from help, your negative self separates you from ideas, activities, emotions, people, and higher forces that could connect you with true power.

Your positive self knows that you are not separate from anyone or anything, because everything in the universe is interconnected. It knows that the Creator and the forces of light are in your heart and by your side at all times. They love you without limit, and they want to help you be fully and joyfully powerful. All you need to do is ask. With a sincere heart and an earnest mind, ask your higher loving forces to support you and guide you in every activity, in every way that furthers your spiritual growth.

Do not let your negative ego trick you into believing that something is too mundane or unimportant to qualify for help. Before you meet with someone, take a trip, begin a project, spend money, solve a problem, perform a ritual, create an opportunity, or go to sleep, ask the higher forces to help you for your highest good. The results will raise the quality of your life and your spirits.

LIFE PRIORITIES

Do you feel confused about life priorities? Do you seem to lack direction? Do you not know what you want? Do you spend too much of your time doing what other people think you should be doing?

Here's a sure-fire way to get all your ducks in a row. Initially it might seem like tough stuff, but there is nothing like it for gaining clarity and igniting motivation. It is essential to your well-being and growth to know what's essential.

Ask yourself what you would do if you were going to die in five years. What changes would you make regarding career, relatives, friends, and lifestyle?

Here's a partial checklist: With whom would you want to spend the most time? With whom the least? Are there relationships that need healing? What steps can you take to make peace? Which relationships would you like to end? What activities would you pursue? Would you take more time off? Is there something you have always wanted to do but keep putting it off? Is there somewhere you have always wanted to go?

What would you keep as it is? Just reaffirming what you would not change can be life enhancing.

If you were going to die in one year, how would your answers be different?

The saying, "Today is the first day of the rest of your life," is simple but true. Without being reckless, irresponsible, or destructive—to yourself or to others—start living as if your life depended on it. Make the choices and implement the changes necessary to bring fulfillment within your grasp. You deserve the best life possible!

THE RIGHT INFO.

OUR subconscious minds are like a universal Internet, linked to each other, the Earth, our supraconscious selves, the universe, and the Creator. This means your subconscious knows what the person you are talking to is thinking and feeling. It knows what babies, animals, and plants need. It knows past and future events because it sees time as whole. It knows how to heal your body.

Your subconscious is ready and willing to relay all this information to your conscious mind, but it usually isn't able. The language of your subconscious is mental imagery, which is a right-brain function, but too often your conscious mind is occupied with verbal and analytical activities in your left brain. Your subconscious receives the equivalent of a busy signal and cannot get through.

To go on-line with your right brain, do right-brain activities. Remember happy emotions. Listen to instrumental music (lyrics are left-brain). Do something like drawing (not writing) with your left hand. Visualize positive images. Daydream. Then ask for information, but not with words. Mentally picture the person, place, or circumstance you want to know about, complete with forms and colors. Give the image your full attention for half a minute or so, letting feelings surface. The energy of your attention signals and stimulates your subconscious.

Your subconscious gathers information from its various sources and sends it to your conscious right brain in the form of sense impressions and a constellation of mental images. Be open and attentive to them, without making left-brain judgments. Always use the information for good, or the bad energy will boomerang back on you. Being in your right mind helps you enjoy the right info.

AVOID THE CRUSH

It is an excellent possibility that everything that happens in our lives—pleasant and unpleasant—is designed to teach us to become more loving and aware. Key experiences are orchestrated by your higher self, which has only your highest good at heart and also has the big picture of your evolution.

Long before you're aware of it, your higher self sees when you are veering off track, spinning your wheels, or are stuck in a dead end of behavior. To help you get traction and get back on track, your higher self sends a lesson to stand politely outside the door of your awareness. The lesson knocks gently. Usually you are too busy keeping your wheels spinning to hear it knocking, or you hear it and tell it to go away, you don't want any lessons today.

The lesson, operating under higher orders than yours, knocks more loudly. You yell at the lesson to beat it. Your yelling interferes with your ability to hear others, and a series of misunderstandings may ensue with unpleasant results.

Each time you reject the lesson, its intensity escalates, becoming louder and more insistent. Your life begins to unravel; more and more events go wrong. Eventually the lesson has no choice but to take an ax to break through the door of your consciousness. It crashes unavoidably into the room of your living in the form of one or more crushing crises—usually involving health or wealth—and pins you to the floor of your life until the pain motivates you to change and grow.

Avoid the crush by being alert to lessons when they first knock politely at your door. Open your awareness wide and invite the lesson in for tea. Serve it a cup of attention sweetened with gratitude. As soon as you become acquainted with the lesson, its presence is no longer required and it departs.

FROM THE HEART

WHAT motivates you to choose one course of action over another? There might seem to be a number of forces at work, but surprisingly they fall into two main categories: negative ego and love.

Within everyone is a negative, ornery, destructive self. Even genuinely enlightened people have such a negative self or ego, but they are able to transcend its influence. Most of us, however, are not yet so aware and resolute, and we are susceptible to the negative ego's siren call. It is very, very, tricky.

The goal of your negative ego is to separate you from love and true power. It seeks your downfall and destruction, but because it is clever it hides its true intent from you. It entices you with visions of physical, financial, and intellectual dominance. It lures you down the pleasure path with excessive drugs, alcohol, sex, and food. Or it convinces you that you are powerless, then uses fear to paralyze you so you are unable to take positive action. Whenever fear, unhealthy pleasure, or thoughts of superiority are part of a decision, consider them to be red flags warning you that your negative ego is at work. Decisions made by your negative ego are doomed to fail sooner or later, because the negative ego operates by first giving you the world, then blowing it up, keeping you off balance, fragmented, and disconnected from love and true power.

The goal of love is more love. Love wants you to be the most joyful, vital, fulfilled, wise, loving, prosperous, and powerful being you can be. When love of self, others, life, work, the Earth, and the Creator motivates your decisions, the results are uplifting and healthy. Decisions made from your heart are fueled by the power of love and are bound to succeed.

RELAX

How much of you is relaxed as you read this? Ninety percent? Fifty percent? Ten percent? Although your body relaxes while you're asleep, there are powerful ways to help it relax when you're awake using the guidance of your conscious mind. Short periods of awake relaxation increase physical and mental energy flow.

Lie down on your back to help take physical pressure off your body and keep your spine and head in alignment. Loosen your clothing. Keep your arms slightly away from your sides, and your legs a comfortable distance apart.

Pull your breath all the way down into your belly two or three times to open up your energy. Then breathe naturally, following the rhythm of your breathing. Put aside distracting thoughts or feelings— they will still be there when you are done, and you can give them stronger, clearer, more focused energy then.

Focus first on your feet. Imagine that each foot is enfolded in a warm, fluffy slipper of golden white light. Your feet relax and absorb the light.

Feel the warm, bright light moving up past your ankles to your knees, surrounding them and soaking into them. Then it moves up to your pelvis and hips, enfolding and filling your abdomen, and soaking into every organ. It rises up to your heart and lungs, and up through your spine. Flowing up through your neck, the light fills your head, melting fears and worries and illuminating your positive thoughts. You are surrounded and filled with light.

As the light flows around and through your body, feel it dissolving tensions and toxins, both physical and emotional, and restoring harmony and vitality.

Thank your body for the twenty-four-hour service it gives you every day of your life. Give it a mini-vacation often; it will return refreshed and more productive.

UNASSUMING

A pundit once quipped, "When you *assume* you make an *ass* out of *u* and *me*." We like to think we know what we are doing, so rather than reveal any uncertainties, we forge ahead without benefit of complete information, sometimes with disastrous results.

Here are some occasions when assuming can make the pundit's observation a reality: Assuming you correctly heard what someone said. Assuming you can predict what someone is going to do or say. Assuming you know what someone wants or needs. Assuming you know how someone is feeling. Assuming that a driver with a flashing right signal light is going to turn right. Assuming the tropics are always hot. You get the idea.

You might assume and be dead to rights wrong. You might pass that car on the left because they're signaling right, and they suddenly turn left right into you. Fortunately, such literal and figurative accidents are easily avoidable. The antidote to assuming is to ask. "Did I correctly understand you to say . . . ?" "Are you planning to . . . ?" "What do you need?" "How are you feeling?"

If you are going to assume anything, assume you don't know. Ask questions. Gather as much information as you can. Do research. The more important the situation, the more important it is to be correctly informed.

It is your negative ego that makes you think that admitting to uncertainty shows weakness, or is embarrassing. The truth is that admitting you don't know takes more courage and strength of character than pretending you know, and it is far less embarrassing than assuming and being wrong. Don't be an ass, ask.

REINFORCEMENTS

Most people have an ornery side that seems to want the exact opposite of whatever they want, if not across the board, at least in some particular area of life. If you are less happy, healthy, wealthy, or loved than you want to be, your ornery side could be blocking success out of hurt or fear.

To turn your resistant self into a cohort, you need to know what it is thinking and feeling. The trouble is, its thoughts and feelings are taking place in your subconscious mind. To raise them to the conscious level, and articulate them, use a positive affirmation. Sometimes it is easier to discover the best one to use by first coming up with its negative opposite. Think about what is really bothering you, what makes you unhappy, or your attitude towards others, your body, work, or the Creator, and write it down. For example, "People always let me down."

Now reverse the statement so it is positive. "People always support me." That's the positive affirmation that will trigger your ornery self to reveal itself to you. On a good-sized pad of paper, write, "People always support me." You will hear a contrary comment in your mind, something like, "Not a chance," or "Get real." Your ill-tempered self has just introduced itself. Acknowledge it by writing down what it says on the line under the affirmation. Now skip a line and write your positive statement again. Write down what your obstinate self says next.

Continue alternately writing your affirmation and your ornery self's comments until its responses agree with your positive statement. Writing the negative responses helps release negative attitudes, and repeatedly reinforcing your affirmation creates positive change. Just as your life reflected the negative belief, so your life will now reflect the new, positive belief.

PLAN AHEAD

THE more clear you are in your mental world about what you want to accomplish in your physical world, the more easily and fully you will realize your goals. This applies whether a goal is large or small, simple or complicated.

At the beginning of each day, think about what you need to do during the day ahead, writing down your key tasks. If there are too many goals to realistically achieve, prioritize in order of importance.

Before important meetings and telephone conversations, make use of the hand-eye-brain triangle of energy and write down what points you want to cover and the results you want to produce. Instead of making a linear left-brain list, try the creative right-brain noting method Tony Buzan suggests in his book, *Using Both Sides of Your Brain*. In the center of a sheet of unlined paper write your central point in one or two words, and put a box or a circle around it. Think of the next important point and write it on a line that branches out from the key point, with related ideas branching out from that point like a tree. Clustering ideas increases the flow of their energy. Or if you like to draw or doodle, sketching simple pictures of you achieving each goal also puts you in your right mind.

What do you want to accomplish by the end of the week? The end of the month? What relationships do you want? Where do you want to be in your life a year from now? Five years? Ten years? Choose how you would most like to die, when and where. Focus on what you want to dream about tonight. Creating a keen mental image of each goal conveys them to your subconscious and supraconscious minds, as well as to your angels, eliciting their energy and assistance. Your life is more likely to go according to plan when you have a plan.

YOU ARE I

1. All life, in whatever form it expresses itself, is energy.
2. All energy is conscious.
3. All energy is part of a whole and is connected.
4. Your view of any aspect of the whole cannot be objective because you are not separate from it.

Such observations on the nature of the universe have been substantiated by physicists in the last 100 years.

These premises hold particular meaning when applied to the people in your life. People are conscious energy in solid, liquid, and gaseous form, as are you, and your energy and theirs are intimately connected on conscious and unconscious levels. When you wholeheartedly and wholemindedly embrace your subjective point of view, you realize that other people are extensions of yourself. You can literally see who you are by looking at the people around you.

The people with whom you have the most emotionally energetic interactions reflect the aspects of yourself which you most need to be aware of. If you know someone who is loving, generous, compassionate and powerful, it is because you are. Being in their presence strengthens the energy of those attributes in yourself, and vice versa. If someone you know limits their choices due to fear, instead of feeling holier-than-thou, look for fear within yourself. By healing your fear you help them heal theirs, because you are connected. People whom you consider enemies, because they seek to harm you on some level, are your greatest teachers because they show you how you harm yourself. Bless them for inspiring you.

Separation from any form of life is an illusion, there is only connection: they are you, you are them, you are I, and I am you.

CELEBRATE SUCCESS

AFFIRM and expand your success consciousness by focusing on every success throughout the day. No success is too small to celebrate.

Begin in the morning by acknowledging your success in getting out of bed. (Some days, getting up is a real accomplishment!) Say to yourself, mentally or aloud, "I am successful in getting out of bed." Proceed from there:

> I am successful in brushing my teeth.
> I am successful in arriving at. . . .
> I am successful in contributing to. . . .
> I am successful in eating lunch.
> I am successful in making this phone call.
> I am successful in solving this problem.
> I am successful in being kind to. . . .
> I am successful in achieving this goal.
> I am successful in arriving home.

Always state your acknowledgment in a short, positive sentence, and *always* in the present tense. It's important to actively think of yourself as a successful person in the here and now, so you can be successful in the future.

As you reinforce both your major and minor successes throughout the day, your subconscious mind really gets the idea that, hey, "I *am* successful!" It will then support that belief by helping you create bigger and better successes.

The more you succeed in thinking you are successful, the more successful you will be, and the more occasions you will have to celebrate!

156

REEL LIFE

IF your life were a movie, you would be producer, director, and star. It is said about movies, "If it isn't on the page, it won't be on the screen," meaning that if the quality of the script is poor, the quality of the movie will be poor, too. To ensure that the quality of your life is excellent, add scriptwriter to your list of job descriptions, and write a top-notch script of your life as you would like it to play on the big screen. You can make it an epic movie that covers the time from the present until your death, or you can narrow the focus to a year, or even a week. Do you want to star in a drama, comedy, thriller, romance, action movie, or a horror picture? It is your choice. What is the title of your life movie?

You, of course, are the central character. What scenes take place to fulfill your needs and wants? What other characters play key roles? Some may already exist, and some you create. What lines do you want to say and hear?

Write it all out—characters, scenes, dialogue—through the last scene, like a narrative script. Write from your heart, especially when your head wants to worry about spelling and syntax. The act of writing creates a circuit of energy that flows from your heart and mind to your hand, which grounds and boosts the energy and sends it back to your brain. Writing gives your subconscious mind a clear idea of the characters, dialogue, action, and props you want in your life. It can then do its job as assistant director more efficiently. The script tells your conscious mind, which is like the camera, what to focus on. Your supraconscious is like the head of the studio, and it can green light the production.

Once you have a script that has both pizzazz and a happy ending, it is time to get busy producing, directing, and starring in your reel life.

LEADING IS SERVING

NOT too long ago, people in positions of leadership expected their followers to follow their lead, and the followers were conditioned to believe that following was part of their job description. For a follower not to follow and a leader not to lead was tantamount to blasphemy, and could jeopardize one's position. Ironically, the separation between leader and follower diminished everyone's capacity to be powerful and effective, because it disconnected their energy.

Progressive businesspeople and other leaders are creating a new model of leadership that more accurately reflects the natural order of the universe where all energy is connected. Many leaders who used to be remote and separate from those they led, are now connecting through attitude and action. Where they once might have allowed their negative egos to run rampant with acquisitions and uncaring power, leaders are redefining their position as being one of service. Rather than keeping followers subservient, leaders are serving their followers by supporting the development of their leadership abilities. The respectful exchange of ideas and energy, and the sharing of skills, expands the powerfulness of everyone involved, creating aliveness and greater success.

Throughout your life, even during a single day, there will be times when you are a leader, and times when you are a follower. You might lead your children, follow a parent, lead a department, follow a boss, lead a friend, follow a teacher, lead the troops, or follow a president. In each role, your purpose is to facilitate the flow of life energy for the greatest good of all concerned. If you block it, you do everyone a disservice, including yourself. A good rule of thumb is to serve those whom you lead, and only follow those who serve.

DOING IT

"I'LL call you." "I'll drop by." "I'll help you." "I'll bring you some soup." "I'll take the kids to the zoo." "I'll take you out to dinner." How many times have you said you would do these things? How many times have you not done them?

An English proverb says, "A person of words, but not of deeds, is like a garden full of weeds." Your intentions are likely to be honorable at the time you extend the offer, but not doing what you say creates unproductive situations on several levels. First it creates awkwardness between you and the other person. Emotionally, you open the door of expectation, but by not walking through it, disappointment arrives instead, leaving the other person standing anxiously at the door. When emotional satisfaction is thwarted, your energy, the other person's, and the energy between you, becomes diminished and agitated. You might also keep in mind that metaphysicists believe that when you die you experience whatever emotions you have produced in others.

By not following through on what you say, you tell your subconscious mind that your words are without meaning; it then disregards them, making your affirmations less effective. More significantly, you instill the belief that you do not want to achieve your goals. Your subconscious supports your beliefs without evaluating them, so it creates weeds, instead of blossoms of success.

These consequences are a high price to pay for not doing what you say. Unless you prefer to continually trip over mental and emotional loose ends, do what you say you are going to do. If you can't, take responsibility by explaining to the person why you are unable to follow through, and apologize.

To not take action is to be powerless. Be powerful; complete your actions.

MENTAL HEALTH

Your mind is a powerful tool. You can use it to hammer problems until you nail the solution; drill into ideas, penetrating their depths; hone innovations; and craft your words. Your mind is the door to your imagination, where you can leap space and time in a single thought. It builds bridges between you and others. It propels your actions. It paves the path leading to the Creator.

Who is in charge of using this tool? Your mind? Think again. A self-aware, self-determining you exists before and after you have a mind. That you self-actualized is not the tool, anymore than you are a screwdriver or a computer. Letting your mind run rampant is as great a folly as letting your television decide what channel to watch. You, not your mind, are the force that determines how well you use your mental tools.

The condition of your mental tools will affect the quality of what you create, because in matters of mind over matter, your mind definitely matters. Your thoughts generate energy, which affects the energy of people, activities, and objects in your physical reality. Broadcasting mental static can actually push away desirable events and opportunities by scattering the energy. Pull whom and what you desire to you by keeping the quality of your thoughts high and harmonious.

The fact that what you think is what you get means that the stronger and healthier your mind is, the more robust your life will be. Your mind's needs are similar to your body's. Feed your mind nutritious positive thoughts about yourself and your world. Keep it fit with mental exercise such as problem solving and creativity. Stimulate it with new information, locales, and experiences. Amplify it with grateful, loving thoughts. Rest it with dreams, day and night. Take good care of your mind and it will remain sharp and well oiled, and last a lifetime.

LIGHT READING

Pᴿᴬᴺᴬ is perhaps the easiest nonphysical reality to see. If you have ever unintentionally "seen" pinpoints of spiraling light in the air, you have experienced an altered state of consciousness, not a malady. Prana is the life-force, a kind of cosmic staple food that nourishes vitality and growth in body, mind, and spirit. Some metaphysicists say that prana comes from another dimension of consciousness and pops into our plane of existence courtesy of the magnetic energy of our sun.

To intentionally see prana, choose a time when it is most abundant, after the sun has been shining for several hours. Places where there are trees and healthy growing green plants also attract plenty of prana. If you live in a city, find a quiet place in a park, or even a balcony full of sunshine and plants will work.

With the sun at your back, sit, lie down, or stand. Pick a piece of clear blue sky and breathe deeply with it. Softly focus your eyes on the sky, then let your gaze drift in toward you until you are aware of the sky but are not looking at it directly. Keep you and your eyes relaxed by breathing slowly and deeply.

When you achieve a state of unlooking seeing, you will begin to notice bright white sparkles of light in the air that float and spin, and gently burst. It may look as if it is snowing prana, but if in your excitement you look sharply at the prana, you will shift back into ordinary reality and lose sight of it.

Breathe in the prana so it can circulate throughout your body. Do this especially after it has been overcast, when prana has been in short supply. A generous serving of this cosmic food every day will help keep your body vigorous, your mind clear, your emotional heart strong, and your spirit willing.

BURNING BELIEFS

BELIEFS range from the mundane to the complex. "I can never find a parking space downtown." "God is punishing me." It doesn't matter whether you acquired your beliefs because you were conditioned by others, or you came to your own conclusions based on observation and experience, a belief is a belief is a belief.

Your subconscious mind accepts all your beliefs at face value, without evaluating their quality, and makes sure your physical reality is consistent with them. Your beliefs about how your world works also close or open the door between you and your higher self. A positive belief opens the door for your supraconscious to help you, but a negative one closes the door.

To open doors and reprogram your subconscious, delete your limiting beliefs and install expansive ones. You can articulate a belief by looking at your physical reality, which is a reflection of your beliefs. An unpleasant pattern of events that occurs repeatedly is a negative belief in action. Write it in a single sentence on a small piece of gray or dark paper, in black ink. "Life is hard." "I never get what I want." "People are selfish." Then say aloud, "I release this limitation." Draw a big thick black X through it. Repeat, "I release this limitation." Rip the paper into pieces. Repeat, "I release this limitation." Now burn the paper (safely), to clear the negative energy of the belief.

On a piece of large white or bright paper, using brightly colored ink, write the opposite of the negative belief. "Life is easy." "I always get what I want." "People are generous." Light a candle in a holder, and place the new belief near it (safely). For ten consecutive days repeat the positive belief aloud three times each day, mentally picturing yourself enjoying your new physical reality.

EAR MASSAGE

YOUR body represents the interconnectedness of life. Each part of your body is connected to every other part through blood and nerves, so that what takes place in one area of your body affects other areas. This is especially true of your hands, feet, head, and ears, which contain energy points that connect to every area of your body. Massaging them benefits your entire system.

Your ears are perhaps the most convenient areas to massage because they are easily accessible and relatively small, so you can rub them almost any place you happen to be. According to reflexologists, there are over a hundred different energy points on your ears that are connected to different areas of your body. Picture your ear like a baby curled upside-down in a fetal position with its head pointed toward your ear lobe, its back curved along the outer edge of your ear, its knees drawn up to its chest, and its top arm resting along its side. These are roughly how the points on your ear relate to your body.

To stimulate a particular part of your body, rub the corresponding point on your ear between the pads of your thumb and forefinger. Be extremely careful not to penetrate the ear canal, and do not use any kind of sharp instrument near your ear. Also, take extra care that your fingernails do not scratch your ear drum.

The health of your ear reflects the health of your body and its organs. To locate sore spots in your body, rub your entire ear from top to bottom. Tenderness in any area can mean the energy is blocked in that part of your body. Massage the tender spot for three minutes to increase energy flow. Gently pulling your ear also helps. Initially your ear will tingle, then become warm. Your body, too, will feel warm and flexible, as if it has been massaged.

NATURAL ART

HAVE you ever noticed how nature seems to be naturally artistic? A daffodil, rocks in a river, an autumn leaf, a meadow full of flowers, an icicle, are all artful. They are an expression of the artistic grace of their Creator.

A direct way to be close to the Creator is to be close to nature. Put yourself near earth, grass, flowers, trees, rocks, or water, or any combination that is available to you. Instead of being a passive observer of nature, deepen the connection by participating creatively in that which the Creator has created. Just as you cannot improve on the color yellow, but you can use yellow in many different ways, the goal here is not to improve on nature, but to be alert to how to use nature's materials in an artful way.

This might mean simply gathering flowers and greens, and taking them home to arrange attractively. Or try your hand and creativity at stacking different sizes, shapes, and colors of stones. Your designs can be passive or kinetic, they might look like miniature Stonehenges, or dragons. Weave dandelions together. Make designs in the snow. Arrange leaves in patterns.

A master of natural art is British artist Andy Goldsworthy, who uses only that which he finds in nature to create his pieces. His book, *A Collaboration with Nature*, inspires with photographs of grass snakes, arches of ice, boulders wrapped in poppy petals, and leaves stitched together with thorns to form horns.

Exploring nature with the eye of an artist opens you to its deeper nature. Touch the earth with aliveness and feel the touch of sun and breeze to put you in touch with yourself and the power of the Creator. By co-creating with nature you remember that you can be a co-Creator in every aspect of your life.

DEFLECTING NEGATIVITY

CERTAIN forms of negative energy are positive and necessary, as in electricity, but the kind of negative energy generated by some people's thoughts and actions is unnecessary, and can be harmful and toxic. It is usually obvious that people who engage in self-destructive activities block or diminish vital energy within themselves and in those around them. Thoughts, too, have impact. Those who are caught in a loop of negative, unkind thinking, can decrease and contaminate your power. People with whom you are in conflict may even intentionally wish you ill.

To deflect negativity, mentally picture yourself surrounded by six one-way mirrors, the reflective sides facing away from you. Picture a mirror in front of you, to your right, behind you, to your left, under your feet, and above your head. You now have 360 degrees of protection, but you can see out as through glass. Mirrors are effective because dark, negative energy does not like to see itself.

If you are angry with a person who wishes you harm, you might be tempted to reflect their negativity right back at them, but this only intensifies and perpetuates the negative energy. Instruct the mirrors, and your guardian angel or spiritual counselor, to send the negativity into the light to be healed.

In cases where someone is generating severe ill will, picture the person surrounded by a box of mirrors, with the reflective sides facing the person. Again, the part of you that has been hurt might want to strike back by having the mirrors return the person's negativity to them, but this only aggravates the situation. Instruct the mirrors to return the person's energy to them in the form of love and light. This helps promote healing and peace, which is the goal.

You are entitled to protect yourself; do so as often as necessary.

FORGIVABLE

UNFORTUNATELY, it is all too likely that somewhere, sometime, someone has hurt you. It might have been through neglect, abuse, deceit, humiliation, betrayal, exploitation, disloyalty, or rejection. If the hurt is still within you, it is causing tension that blocks energy on every level, causing many varieties of dis-ease. Forgiving the other person eases tension on all levels, allowing the energy to flow, and bringing health and harmony to body, mind, heart, and spirit.

The paths that lead to forgiveness can be challenging. If the harmful action was severe and repeated, you become attached to your resentment, outrage, and grief because they are justified. With the help of a therapist, you can release the pain that keeps you glued to anger. If you are waiting for the person to compensate you for the hurt they caused, or apologize, such expectations tie up energy you could be putting to good use elsewhere in your life. It helps to understand that the person's unkind behavior was in direct proportion to how disconnected from their power they were, and they wanted you to be powerless, too. Continuing to feel powerless traps you in victimhood. Fortunately the entry point to power is always in the present moment, because you have the power of choosing what you do right now.

Forgiving the person is taking positive action which reconnects you to your power. Visualize yourself and the person in a beautiful natural setting, each of you surrounded by a ball of bright white light. Say out loud, "I release you (person's name) and all pain and injury, into the light of the Creator to be healed. I (your name) forgive you (person's name)." Repeat it as many times as it takes to genuinely feel what you are saying. Forgive yourself for holding onto the hurt. When you are able to forgive, you are able to live.

FREE SPEECH

IN democratic countries people are guaranteed freedom of speech. Short of threatening the life of the head of state or the overthrow of the government, accusing someone falsely, making slanderous remarks, or yelling "Fire!" in public places when there is no fire, people are allowed to speak up and out about any topic, issue, or problem to bring about change.

Sadly, regardless of the political climate in which they live, many people behave as if they had a dictator within them who forbids them to speak up about their problems, feelings, or needs. If you are among those who submit to the dictates of an inner despot for fear you will be punished or humiliated if you speak your mind and heart, you are living in a state of disempowerment.

It is time to overthrow the tyrant. It does not have to be a dramatic Boston Tea Party sort of rebellion to be successful. Simple acts are liberating. Begin by speaking honestly to yourself. Admit you are having a problem and describe it, aloud or in writing. When you have acted contrary to how you felt, articulate your true feelings. "I acted as if I were fine, but I felt hurt, angry, lonely, confused." Define your needs. When you can speak up to yourself about yourself, it is much easier to do it with someone else.

Speak up and out honestly with others. Ask for help. Be clear about your feelings and needs. Let people know the impact their words and actions—or lack of them—have on you. You have every right to speak freely, but not unkindly. The risk of discomfort is worth the help, comfort, insight, increased self-esteem, and improved quality of life you stand to gain when you speak your truth. Live in a state of empowerment. Freedom of speech helps make you free.

WORRIER WARRIOR

ARE you an equal opportunity worrier or a worrier warrior? Do you worry every chance you get, about everything, large and small. If you have an extra few minutes, do you worry about what you did or didn't do, and what you will or will not get done? Do you really come alive at night as soon as your head hits the pillow? Do you worry about money, your health, something you did ten years ago, the motives and behaviors of those you know, and the end of the world?

Worries are thoughts that are stuck in the mud of negative energy; you're spinning your mental wheels but you're not going anywhere. To worry without taking action is to be powerless, and it uses up a great deal of your energy that could be put to more constructive use. Become a worrier warrior and take control of your worries instead of letting worries control you. First, acknowledge that you are worrying. As soon as you name what you are doing you begin to take back your power. Next, write down everything you are worried about, in no particular order. Worries that seem to swarm like a black cloud of killer bees, may surprisingly be reduced to three flies and a mosquito on the page. Defining them reduces their numbers and makes them less menacing, which makes them more manageable. Determine which worries are legitimate and which are merely nuisances. Or worse, is your mind entertaining itself because it has nothing better to occupy it? Number your worries in order of importance. Start with the most pressing worries and identify what actions you can take to reduce a particular problem, or eliminate it all together. Resolve to give your mind more substantial, positive food to chew on.

The list of worries becomes your shield against powerlessness. Your sword is forged with the actions you take. You are a warrior against worry.

LOVE TO SPARE

No matter how busy you are, one or two not-so-busy minutes fall into your lap here and there throughout the day. It can happen when you are on hold on the telephone, waiting for an elevator, riding in a taxi or bus, standing in line at the post office or the supermarket, stopped at a red light, waiting for a computer to boot up, or walking from point A to point B.

Instead of fussing impatiently because something is taking longer than you would like it to, and getting your energy all in a lather, use that spare minute or two to do something that expands and harmonizes your energy. Become aware of your breathing and take a few even, deep breaths. Bring your attention more fully into the present by noticing as much about yourself and your immediate environment as you can. Feel your heart beating. Hear your breathing. Feel your clothes on your body, your shoes on your feet. Feel where your body is in contact with the floor or the ground. What sounds do you hear? What aromas do you smell? What do you see? If there is a goal you are working toward, vividly and joyfully visualize yourself achieving it. Picture a ball of bright light around you. Or feel grateful for someone or something, including yourself.

Turn you attention and energy to others. Picture balls of bright white light around those you love. Especially picture light around those you do not love, they may very well be your teachers. If someone you know is ill or injured, or is facing challenges, say a prayer for them that they receive the love, help, and strength they need. Or if someone is working towards a goal, visualize them achieving it, feeling as glad for their success as you do for your own. Use your spare time to love yourself and others, and you will have love to spare.

LISTEN UP

Some pundits have said that the Creator gives us one mouth and two ears because we are supposed to listen twice as much as we talk. Unfortunately, most of us do the opposite; we talk twice as much as we listen. Some people use talking to erect a wall of words to hide behind so they remain separate.

Listening strengthens connections with others, yourself, and the Creator. It is one of the primary ways we gather information, but by not spending more time on the receiving end of a conversation we miss many great opportunities for learning. Listening does not mean paying silent lip service to not talking. True listening is something you do actively, with aliveness and awareness. You pay attention not just by keeping your ears open, but also your mind and heart. Ironically, you also listen better if your mouth is slightly open—but not moving!

Make the time and effort to listen to everyone. Listen to a troubled friend. You don't have to try to fix their problems, but you can offer needed comfort by listening empathetically to how they feel. Listen to your parents as human beings in their own right. Listen to children as they discover their world. Listen to what people at work need. Listen to the waitress, the dentist, the plumber, the banker, the homeless person. Anyone can be your teacher if you allow them.

Listen to the wind, a river, a tree spirit; each has a voice and knowledge. Listen to the rhythm of your heart, your breath. Listen to how your body feels and what it needs. Listen to your intuition. Listen to your angels. Above all—pun intended—listen to the Creator, which speaks through all creation. There is a whole wise universe out there and in there, from which to learn. Listen.

GOLDEN SHINE

"**D**o unto others as you would have others do unto you."

Perhaps your reaction to the Golden Rule is: "Other people don't treat me the way I want to be treated, so why should I treat them well?" Refusing to act lovingly because you have been hurt in the past and are now keeping score, creates heavy, dull energy within you and around you. Surrounding yourself with such negative energy does not inspire others to act lovingly towards you and can actually deflect kindness. When you behave towards others in ways you would not like yourself, that negative energy boomerangs back on you, often in harsher ways than your initial act.

Tear up your "Who Has Been Nice To Whom" scorecard. The beauty of living the Golden Rule is that it generates a rich, shining river of positive energy that flows within you, around you, between you and others, from others to others, and between you and the Earth and the Creator. Treat others with kindness, respect, generosity, and honesty, and those qualities will flow back to you, although it is not always those to whom you are kind, who are kind to you.

In every situation, personal and business, consider what you need and want, then do that for the others involved. What do the people around you need: materially, emotionally, spiritually? What would light them up, bring comfort, help them grow? During a conflict, what is the fair action to take? How can you help create win/win outcomes? Let integrity be the true mettle of your actions.

Expand the Golden Rule to include all life-forms: people, animals, plants, the Earth, the universe, angels, and the Creator. Treat all life as you want to be treated—with love, consideration, gratitude, and respect—and the world, both physical and metaphysical, will reciprocate in kind, and then some!

COLOR ME SLEEPY

THERE is a more uplifting way to pull the wool over your eyes at night than counting sheep. Several hours ahead of time, choose the hour by which you want to be asleep, and visualize yourself happily asleep in your bed with your bedside clock displaying the time you've chosen. Reinforce the image once every hour until lift-off. Avoid eating heavy or sugary foods, or large amounts of food, for at least three hours before bedtime so your body is not busy digesting.

Once in bed, lie on your back and close your eyes. Picture or sense yourself wrapped head to toe in a blanket of soft gleaming white light, then place your hands around your abdomen and breathe the light deeply into the bowl of your belly. Exhale tensions and worries into the light around you. Stress might look like gray smoke coming out, which the white light absorbs and heals.

Focus on your tailbone and picture the blanket of light around you turning a bright, beautiful red. Exhale physical tension into the red light around you. Move your focus up your spine behind your bellybutton and see the blanket turning orange. Exhale pessimism. Focus on your spine behind your solar plexus and be surrounded in yellow. Exhale worries into it. Focus on your spine behind your heart, as you are wrapped in vibrant green. Exhale emotional fears and pain into the green light. Focusing on the back of your neck, think blue. Give blue the words you haven't said, but wanted to. Focus a couple of inches behind the center of your forehead and picture violet light all around you. Exhale selfishness. Focus on the top of your head and the blanket is once again white, protecting you through the night. Repeat as needed. Being enveloped in a rainbow of colors and exhaling tensions make for colorful dreams. Why fall asleep when you can rise?

MIND BANK

It can be said that your brain functions as both a transmitter and receiver, continually broadcasting and receiving thoughts. How is it that thoughts can travel? A simple explanation is that the electricity of thoughts generates waves of energy, which have motion and so travel. These waves of energy carry thoughts, just as radio waves carry words and music. Some thoughts are known to you consciously, and some are sent and received on the subconscious level. Whether conscious or unconscious, thoughts have impact when they are received.

You can put this phenomenon to good use whenever you have an important goal you want to achieve, whether it's to be promoted or to be more fit. Contact three or four people whom you know care about you and want the best for you. Help them create a clear mental picture of you having achieved your goal, and ask them to reinforce the image of you succeeding whenever they think of you. It's important that they really put their hearts into it, if only for a few seconds. Receiving their positive thoughts and energy, whether consciously or unconsciously, will strengthen your willingness and ability to achieve your goal.

Do the same for each of them, wholeheartedly picturing each person achieving the success they desire. You could form a "Mind Bank" group whose members invest positive thoughts in each other. Groups of people who share a common goal, such as families, business departments, or sports teams, can also unify their energy by mentally focusing on the same goal. Thinking well of one another produces synergistic dividends, because more can be accomplished through the group energy than might be achieved by each individual alone.

GREAT BALLS OF LIGHT

LIGHT is powerful stuff to have around. What light do you have around you? In addition to physical light, every particle and wave of the metaphysical variety of light around you is beneficial. It illuminates, raises energy levels, dissolves negative energy, promotes personal growth, heals, protects, increases mental clarity, harmonizes vibrations, and connects you with the Creator.

You already have the electricity to turn the light on—your mind. Simply by visualizing yourself surrounded by bright white light—white being the blend of all spectrums of color—you make it so. Your subconscious mind believes that mental images are real and manifests them on the appropriate level.

First, ground yourself by picturing yourself standing outdoors in a beautiful place in nature. About ten feet in front of you, picture a large ball of bright white light that is a little taller and wider than you are. Thank the light for being present with you. Walk right into the center of the light, or invite it to embrace you, or a combination of the two, so you are completely surrounded by the light.

Invite the light to fill you. It may come in through your heart, eyes, hands, belly, the top of your head, or through your skin. Allow it to flow throughout your body, filling your head, brain, neck, chest, heart, arms, hands, abdomen, all your organs, legs, and feet. Everywhere the light goes it absorbs tensions and toxins, be they physical or emotional, and it restores health, harmony, and vitality.

As there is an infinite supply of light, there is plenty to surround everyone and everything. Visualize balls of light around others, your home and office, any vehicle you're in, and the Earth. Place a ball of light in doorways to filter out negative energy of anyone who enters. This is great to do anywhere anytime!

HELP

SOMETIMES events occur, to you or someone you care about, which are so grave or massive you feel totally overwhelmed. Death, cancer, divorce, loss of job, and natural disasters can make you feel utterly helpless. Your sense of powerlessness can be so acute that you begin to think that your whole life is an effort in futility, and that nothing you do is going to make a difference.

The truth is that everything you do makes a difference. When it seems as if it doesn't, that is the time when help needs to become a major part of your consciousness and your vocabulary, as a verb, as a noun, and in the imperative.

Help yourself and others in whatever ways you can. It does not matter how small the action seems compared to the enormity of the problem; as long as it is constructive, it helps. The combined effects of seemingly insignificant positive actions add up to significant change.

Ask for help from others. Be specific. People may have the sincerest of intentions, but they are not mind readers; they need to know what you want and need. Let in the help—you deserve it simply because you are part of creation.

If you feel as if you have reached a dead end, with nothing left to do, no place left to go, no one left to turn to, what do you do then? Turn to higher forces for help. From your deepest pain and sorrow ask your guardian angel, your higher self, and the Creator for guidance and strength. Insist that they help. It is even possible that they allowed the catastrophe to be created to lead you to open the spiritual door and turn to them. Moving through the spiritual door, heart first, re-connects you with authentic, loving power. It is from the spiritual forces that miracles come. Help. Do it! Receive it! Request it!

SILENCE SHINES

SILENCE is indeed golden—physically, mentally, emotionally and spiritually—but its value has lost its luster amidst the din of modern living. Due to technology, ours is the noisiest civilization that ever lived on the planet. We are constantly inundated with the sounds generated by telephones, televisions, movies, stereos, radios, and computers. Factor in the stressful sounds of traffic, construction, airplanes, barking dogs, noisy neighbors, or crying children, and you have Noise.

In this sea of sounds it is possible to create a peaceful island of silence. *Webster's Dictionary* defines being silent as "free from sound or noise." This means no talking or listening to music, although the sounds of nature such as birds, a river, or the wind are permissible. Being silent can also include being still.

To create a truly silent space usually requires physically removing yourself from others. You might withdraw into a quiet room, go to a religious center, or to a peaceful place outdoors. Even sitting in a parked car in the rain can work.

Once you are in a quiet environment, sit cross-legged, or in a comfortable chair with your back supported. When you are physically still, become mentally still. Breathe deeply. At first, your conscious mind will be very active, because its job is to observe and comment on everything, even silence. Just let your thoughts pass by without following them. Focus on each breath you inhale and exhale. Listen to the silence between your thoughts, between your breaths.

Plan some period of silence on a regular basis. Even just five minutes of silence a day will reward you with greater clarity, calm, and energy.

Carry the experience of silence within you, like a steady golden light, in all that you do. Let the peace and strength of silence shine through you to others.

ENERGY BALL

THIS technique might seem mysterious at first, but it really works! It's especially effective for strengthening parts of your body that are weak, injured, or ill. It has even been known to fix electrical systems in cars and computers.

Stand with your feet shoulder-width apart. Hold your hands about ten inches apart in front of your solar plexus, the area just below your heart. Turn the palms of your hands toward each other, curving your fingers as if you were holding a baseball in each hand with the balls facing each other. Stiffen your fingers, but don't straighten them, keeping them curved as if around a ball.

Keeping your fingers curved, stiff, and slightly separated, move your hands in small circles, almost as if each hand were wrapping yarn around a ball of wool, or you were using an eggbeater with balls for handles. The circles should be made quickly and continuously.

As you move your hands in alternating small circles, you'll begin to feel a ball of energy form between your hands. It only takes about a minute to begin to feel the energy. It might feel like a subtle pressure against your fingers and palms, or it might feel tingly or warm. The more rapidly you circle your hands, the stronger and larger the energy becomes. Increase the distance between your hands to accommodate the ball of energy as it expands.

When the ball of energy feels large and powerful, throw it into the part of your body that needs it, or into the engine of your car, or into your computer. At the moment you throw the ball of energy, mentally picture your body, car, or computer as completely healthy and functioning properly. In some cases you will feel or see positive results almost immediately.

LOVED

LEARNING to be loved is a breeze, right? You sign up for the course in the Earth school in which you have enrolled, because it will be a snap, a no-brainer. After all, what could be more natural than being loved?

Guess again. Learning to be loved is perhaps the toughest course life has to offer. Love requires you to be completely open and thoroughly vulnerable, which can be a scary prospect, especially if you are someone who usually tries to control situations. The irony is that the need to be in control is born of fear, and fear is born of lack of love. An easy way to be in control of being loved is to close yourself to it. Ask yourself if it is more important to you to be in control, or to be loved? The choice is always yours. Try giving yourself permission to be loved by writing it several times as an affirmation: "I give myself permission to be loved."

Being loved is like being a cup into which your lover pours love. Is your cup filled with old, dried coffee grounds? Picture yourself washing it out. How big is your cup? It is possible that in the past a lover gave you only a teaspoon of love, leaving you feeling empty and hurt. Your reaction might have been to make your cup smaller. Increase your capacity for love by making your cup bigger.

Lovers are present, in myriad forms, waiting for you to receive their gifts. The Creator knows you wholly, loves you, and pours life into you. Your guardian angel loves you always, in all ways. The earth loves you and feeds you. The air just waits for you to breathe in its life. The sun loves you. Plants love you. If you are especially fortunate, you know people who love you and animals who love you. The more you become aware of all the ways the universe loves you, and allow yourself to receive that love, the more your cup will spill over with love.

PEACE WITHIN AND WITHOUT

THAT anything happens "out there" is an illusion created by believing that what happens outside the boundaries of your skin is separate from you. It isn't. It may be distinct in the same way that your liver is distinct from your heart, which is distinct from your brain, but they are all part of the same system. Your body is a metaphor for the connectedness of all life.

Likewise, what happens anywhere on Earth belongs to the same system of energy to which you belong. The ocean may be distinct from the land, China may be distinct from Peru, but they are all part of the same system. The Earth, too, is a metaphor for the connectedness of all life within the Divine energy.

When people become disconnected from life due to pain or anger, violence occurs. Violence is anti-life and anti-love. Because we all belong to the same system of energy, violence anywhere on the planet is a wake-up call to our having separated ourselves from the power of life, love, and the Creator. Violence can manifest in the form of a person such as Attila the Hun or Hitler, or as violent weather, earth upheavals, crime, domestic abuse, or self-abuse. The forms that violence takes may be different, but they are all reflections of inner confusion and separation.

To create peace in the world, first create peace in the world within your heart. Breathe deeply into your heart. Visualize your heart filled with white light. Love who you are—your angels do. Know that the Creator loves you always and completely. Express love to those around you. Take action to upgrade life and eliminate crime in your neighborhood. Embrace life with love, and life will embrace you with love. The more people there are who create peace within, the more peace will manifest without, which is really within.

RETURNING POWER

IT is easy to identify a genuinely powerful person. They appear self-possessed, loving, and joyful. Being around them makes you feel more peaceful, powerful, and happy. If you are not in touch with your power, you might covet the other person's power and try to take some of it for yourself. You might do it consciously, but more often than not you do it unconsciously.

Your negative self, concerned with getting what it needs, thinks that taking another person's energy is a good idea. It isn't. The Creator gives everyone all the power they need to lovingly live their lives. When you take someone else's power, you have immediately offended the Creator and created discord in this essential relationship. That dissonance reverberates through everything you think, feel, say, and do, causing all your actions to be out of alignment. Your physical life becomes a mirror of your conflict with the Creator.

By taking another person's power you prevent them from using it to learn and grow. You then become responsible to that person for whatever ways you have prevented their fulfillment. Your energy is bound with theirs though time and space, until you return it. Ask your guardian angel to show you mental images of people whose power you have taken, then picture yourself and the person standing in a beautiful place in nature. Ask your guardian angel to take each person's power from you as a ball of light, and return it to its rightful owner. Look each person in their eyes, and apologize, asking them to forgive you. Ask the Creator for forgiveness. Do this with each person whose power you have taken.

The best way to avoid taking power from another is to connect with your own power and learn to use it lovingly as the Creator intended.

PSYCHOMETRY

WOULD you believe that holding someone's plastic comb can tell you if the person is an optimist, has a headache, likes to dance, or is going to receive good news? It can. One hundred and fifty years ago you would have been equally skeptical if you were told that holding a molded piece of plastic against your ear was going to allow you to hear a person talking a thousand miles away.

The system of psychometry is similar to the telephone system. You hold an object belonging to another person and receive information through it. A person initiates a call by giving you something that he or she alone handles frequently: a wallet, a set of keys, or perhaps a ring. Because all matter is energy, the person's energy has mingled with the energy of the object. When you hold the object, its energy directly connects you to the person's energy, and your subconscious mind to their subconscious mind.

To make sure you have a good connection, close your eyes and picture the person whose object you hold, breathing deeply several times. Visualize the two of you surrounded in a bubble of white light, and ask the light to open you to receive only information that is for the person's highest good. Whether standing or sitting, keep you body in an open posture—feet, legs, and arms uncrossed—with your spine straight. You may hold the object in either hand, or both.

Your breathing and focus create a strong, clear connection through all the cosmic chatter. Your subconscious mind, now directly linked to the other person's, transmits past, present, and future information to your conscious mind in the form of sense impressions, mental images, or sounds and words. You then verbally relay the information to the person, completing the circuit.

CRYSTALLIZING

CENTURIES ago healers and shamans throughout the world discovered that certain stones had the power to affect their moods, energy levels, and various areas of their bodies. To better benefit from the stones' effects, they tied them to different parts of their bodies with sinew or plant fibers to hold them close for long periods. Over time, this process was refined and became jewelry.

Precious and semi-precious gemstones are minerals with crystalline structures that can focus, store, transmit, and amplify energy. Quartz is probably the most well known for this because of its use in radio transmitters. It contains silicon, as do our bodies, which may explain the mutual affinity.

To receive the energy of a crystal or gemstone, hold it in your left hand. This helps you and the crystal to become attuned to each other. To focus the energy of a crystal on a particular region of your body or another person's, hold it in your right hand. Crystals also affect rooms in which they are placed. Periodically cleanse and recharge crystals by soaking them in seasalt water until they no longer feel clammy.

Use gemstones to help keep energy crystal clear and balanced. Here is a short guide, with the part of the physical body affected at the end.

- Diamond: Most pure. Breaks up negativity. Amplifies energy. Clears mind.
- Amethyst: Raises vibrations. Balances mind. Protective. Blood.
- Emerald: Aligns energy. Enhances dreams. Deepens spiritual. Strengthens heart.
- Turquoise: Creativity. Communication. Friendship. Throat.
- Clear quartz: Full spectrum energy. Emotions. High self. Brain.
- Opal: Colors resonate with chakras. Deepens intuition. Eyesight.
- Sapphire: Clears confusion. Psychic abilities. Peace. Glands.
- Ruby: Refines coarse energy. Strengthens immune system. Blood.

INTENTION RESOLVE

INTENTION is as essential to power as a driver is to a car. Without intention, your potential sits idle. Without intention, you have no key with which to unlock possibilities or start your engine. Without intention, you lack direction.

The first step toward revving up your intention is to decide what you intend to do, and write it down in a simple positive sentence. "I intend to buy (or build) a house." Then define why you want to do it. "I want my family to have a safe place to live, and room to grow." Be honest. "I want a home for my family that will appreciate in value and will increase their respect for me."

When you are clear about your purpose, your intention is in gear. It engages your physical, mental, emotional, and spiritual energies, and it puts them in sync with each other. Intention is also the high octane energy that fuels your actions so you can move forward more efficiently. It puts you in the driver's seat.

If you only partially define your goal or your purpose, you might find yourself in the car, but drive around in circles because you don't know which direction to go in. When your intention is completely focused you have power steering and can drive yourself exactly where you want to go.

Your body will let you know when your intention has engaged the energy on all levels of your being. You feel as if you are pulling energy up from the earth and down from the heavens to meet in your heart. Your solar plexus and stomach feel strong and bright, and your mind feels alert and clear. You know with absolute certainty that you can accomplish your goal. You are determined.

Resolve to have intention. The stronger your intention is, the greater your success will be, because the energy acts as a magnet to attract what you need.

FREE OF PAIN

IMAGINE this: All the emotions you engender in others, *you* experience. Some people who have had Near Death Experiences (NDE's) have reported that such is the case, that they not only reviewed the events of their lives, but experienced the emotions they caused others to feel, both the joy and the pain.

You have caused pain if your actions have produced physical, mental, emotional, or spiritual distress of any intensity or duration, in another. Make a list of people you have taken advantage of, lied to, stolen from, hit, neglected, defamed, harmed, manipulated, belittled, or killed. The people you've hurt might include parents, siblings, other relatives, friends, lovers, spouses, children, coworkers, bosses, employees, partners, customers, strangers, or neighbors.

If the person to whom you have caused distress is alive and you are in communication with them, take physical action. Call them, write them, visit them. Tell them you want to heal the pain between you. Ask how you made them feel. Listen with your whole being, without defending yourself. Apologize from your heart. Ask for their forgiveness. Ask what you can do to repair the damage. Ask for forgiveness from the Creator. Forgive yourself for the weakness and need that caused you to cause pain to another.

If communication with the person is completely closed, or you do not know where the person is, or they are dead, take metaphysical action. In your mind, visualize yourself sitting with them in a bright, familiar setting, then say all the things you would say if they were physically present. Ask for forgiveness.

You cannot undo the actions that caused pain, but you can mend the consequences of them. Don't wait. Heal the pain now and be free of it.

ANGEL ALERT

You have a guardian angel who is with you from before you draw your first breath, until after you draw your last. If you are involved in activities that uplift others, you undoubtedly have additional angels who are specialists in healing, spiritual leadership, counseling, communication, and so forth.

Your angels possess valuable insights about you, your life purpose, your everyday needs, and what you need for fulfillment. Because they want you to reach your spiritual best, they are eager to share their wisdom with you. Angels can help you even if you do not believe in them, but being open to the possibility of their existence helps them help you more. Out of respect for your free will, they wait for you to ask to receive their guidance before sharing it with you. Once you have asked your angels for their help, be alert to its arrival.

Angels are conscious, loving forces of light, with no attachment to a particular gender or appearance. Their influence can appear in your life in any shape, size, style, or color, but they usually choose forms to which you will be receptive. Angelic messages can come through anyone or anything at anytime. You might be drawn to a book or magazine, and open it to a page with just the information you are looking for. A friend could mention something that has significance for you. Or you find yourself sitting next to a stranger who tells you something that strikes a chord of truth within you. The messenger might be male or female, young or old, rich or poor, urbane or rustic, so do not let your conscious mind limit you by making critical judgments. Angelic forces use whatever is near you to express themselves: a bird, a dream, a river, a song, a flower. An angelic message could be around the next corner, or the next moment. Be alert!

HAND SWITCH

HAVE you ever tried to write with your other hand? It probably felt awkward and you stopped, but there are valuable unconscious insights to be gained by writing with your opposite hand. Switching hands seems to bypass the analytical, verbal left brain, and plugs you into your imaginative, intuitive right brain. Surprisingly, this works for both right-handed and left-handed people.

What usually happens when you try to switch your writing hand is that your negative ego makes it difficult for you to do something new because it does not want you doing anything that might make you more powerful. To trick your "nego," hold a smooth, solid object in the hand with which you usually write. This grounds your normal writing hand and gives it something to occupy its attention. The object might be a stone, a shell, a crystal, or be made of glass or metal.

Have several good-sized sheets of paper on hand, and hold a pen or pencil in the hand that isn't holding an object. Before beginning to write, let go of any agendas about the content, and don't be concerned about penpersonship. Surround yourself with bright white light and ask that whatever is for your highest good come through. Breathe deeply, then let the information pour forth from your angels or High Self, through your subconscious right mind, to your left brain hemisphere to pick up words, then flow down into your hand. The information could come in the form of a letter to you, or you might find yourself drawing pictures and symbols. Do not analyze what you are doing because it will put your focus in your left brain and stop the flow through your right brain.

Switching writing hands throws open a mental switch that allows creative insights, solutions, and ideas to enter your conscious mind. Treasure them.

HEALING ENERGY

Your body may feel solid, especially when it is ill, but that is because you experience it with your left brain from the physical plane. Your right brain and your spirit see the spaces between all those quadrillions of vibrating body molecules as being filled with energy. To your subconscious and supraconscious minds, energy is what is real.

Mental images, emotions, and spiritual light are also energy that is alive and aware. Combining different energies to work together synergistically, produces greater results than any one energy alone, enhancing whatever physical measures you are taking to improve your health. To help heal the energy of your body with higher energy, visualize your body being filled and surrounded by loving white light. In areas of your body that hurt, or where you hold tension, picture the light being extra bright. Feel how caringly the light flows into every cell, reminding its consciousness to be harmonious and healthy. Light is symbolic of the Creator.

In Tantric Yoga, developed in India around the sixth century A.D. to offset the trend of emphasizing the material over the spiritual, practitioners view physical illness as blocked energy. To help energy flow, they project images of specific shapes and colors into afflicted areas of the body. For example, a circle signifies heaven, unity, and the sun. A triangle connects heaven and earth. A spiral is evolution and spirit. Red is birth, mother, and heat. Yellow is light, air, and intuition. Green is earth, fertility, and growth. Blue is sky, thought, and devotion. Violet is spirituality. Ask your body what shape and color it needs in what areas to become healthy. Sense the answers intuitively, then combine the appropriate shapes and colors, focusing their healing energy in specific areas to help good health flow.

187

LIVELY CONVERSATIONS

IF you only exhaled, or only inhaled when you breathed, you would die. The same holds true for conversations. If you only exhale words by talking, or only inhale words by passively listening, the conversation will suffocate.

To converse means to have words *with*, not talk at. Instead of dominating a conversation by doing all the talking, breathe life into your conversations by alternately exhaling and inhaling information. Exhale, talking about yourself or a subject of mutual interest, then encourage the other person to talk, and inhale information about them. When the other person does the same, voilà, the conversation is breathing. It is alive and well. In this way, interesting and helpful information can be exchanged, increasing closeness.

To help a conversation breathe deeply, instead of thinking about what you want to say next when someone is speaking, listen with full attention. Questions about what they are saying will surface naturally. You might not understand something they said and want more clarity, or a point they made interests you and you want to explore it further with them. Author Truman Capote once said that he never found anyone to be boring, because he believed that every person had a unique story to tell, and the process of discovery was itself interesting.

A conversation that breathes also stimulates the yin and yang energy within you, and between you and the other person. You express yang, or masculine energy, when you talk, and you express yin, or feminine energy, when you listen, because you are receiving information. Achieving a yin/yang balance in conversation enhances mental, emotional, and physical vitality. You will feel more alive when your conversations are alive.

FEEL THE EARTH MOVE

Do you want to feel *real* power?

Feel the Earth move.

American engineer extraordinaire, R. Buckminster Fuller, viewed the planet Earth as a giant spaceship hurtling through space. He devised this method for experiencing the power of the Earth's motion.

About half an hour or an hour before the sun sets, go outside to a wide open space with no buildings or trees around it. If the area is big and clear enough to see the curve of the Earth against the horizon, even better. A park, the beach, a large clearing in a forest, or a meadow, are esthetically ideal, but a ballpark, large parking lot, or a vacant lot, will do just as well.

Stand facing north. Spread your feet apart slightly wider than shoulder width. The wider apart they are the more you will feel the motion of the Earth.

Stretch your arms out parallel to the ground, one palm facing the sky, the other palm turned toward the Earth. Without looking directly at the sun, look over your left shoulder toward the west. Catch the sun out of the corner of your eye.

You will feel the magnificent movement of the Earth as it rotates on its axis and revolves around the sun at the same time. If you get a bit dizzy, it's worth it to feel the Earth supporting you and holding you securely to her while hurtling through the vastness of space.

You might think that experiencing such an awesome movement would make you feel insignificant. On the contrary, it inspires and uplifts you. You realize that you are part of a glorious and powerful natural wonder that is itself part of the glorious and natural wonder of the universe.

DRUM HEARTBEAT

In addition to the primary purpose of a ceremony or ritual, the underlying purpose of its various activities is to stimulate the senses, clear energy, focus intention, open the gates to the power of the subconscious and supraconscious minds, and invoke the assistance of spirit guides, angels, and the Creator.

Sound plays a profoundly important role because the wave frequencies of sounds affect your physical energy, your chakra energy centers, and your brain waves. The drum has been used in ceremonies for thousands of years because of the resonance of its beat, and for its symbolic power. To shamans and medicine people in native tribes throughout the world, the circular shape of the drum symbolizes the earth and the oneness of all life forms within the circle of life. The two sides of a drum represent the duality of the physical plane, and the male and female principles. Usually the tone of one side is lower, connecting to the earth. The higher tone connects to the sky and the cosmos.

Shamans use the repetitious beat of the drum to achieve altered states of consciousness, and scientists have confirmed that the rhythm of a drum causes your brain to produce alpha and theta brain waves that heighten awareness and creativity. The rhythm also helps bring the left and right brain hemispheres into harmony. The beat of the drum is a heartbeat that connects your heart with the heart of the Earth. Indeed, the electromagnetic waves of the Earth are about seven cycles per second, which are in the same four-to seven-cycle range as theta brain waves.

Beat a drum before beginning prayers, a meditation, a visualization, or any ritual, allowing your instincts to guide the pattern of your rhythm. When your mind and heart march to the rhythm of a drum, you are in step with power.

WITH YOUR COMPLIMENTS

IN this era of fast faxes and E-mail, snail mail holds an almost old-fashioned charm. When you see a hand-addressed letter among the bills and junk mail, your heart leaps in anticipation. You know that someone has cared enough to make the effort to write you, and it makes you feel special.

Care enough to make the effort on your behalf. Write yourself a letter as if you were writing to your best friend, which you are. Be sure to write it in longhand to take full advantage of the fact that what you write by hand is immediately transmitted to your brain and imprinted on your subconscious mind, which then bases its activities on the information. Writing the letter by hand also makes it more personal. You deserve the best, so use your best stationery.

Beginning with a salutation, "Dear (your name)," proceed to tell yourself how wonderful you are. Don't be shy about it. Don't hold back. It becomes an ego trip only if you compare yourself to others, saying that you are more wonderful than other people. As long as you avoid comparisons, acknowledging your good qualities is positive because it strengthens your self-esteem. This letter is for your eyes only, so you can say whatever you want.

Encourage yourself. Emphasize how well you are doing given certain limits. Commend yourself for specific jobs well done, both professionally and personally. Also give yourself credit for your accomplishments on mental, emotional, and spiritual levels. Perhaps you disciplined yourself to think more positively, or took an emotional risk, or made contact with your guardian angel in a dream. Give yourself verbal pats on the back, then mail yourself the letter. Read it with delight when it arrives, and save it. Compliments complement you.

SPIRIT PROTECTION

Aᴄᴄᴏʀᴅɪɴɢ to the laws of physics, energy changes form but is not destroyed. Water changing from ice, to liquid, to vapor is an example. The same law applies when the physical body dies. The energy that enlivened the body changes form, but it is not destroyed. It remains self-aware and self-determining.

Some people think the conscious energy that continues to exist after physical death, is automatically enlightened simply by virtue of the fact that it is no longer restricted by a physical body. However, sages and metaphysicists believe that the energy continues to express the same traits it did in the physical body. People who were compassionate and helpful to others on the physical plane, go on to express that energy in higher nonphysical realms. People who were mean and harmful, continue the pattern after death, and because their low energy keeps them bound to the Earth plane, they seek out physical prey.

Take precautions. Protect yourself against opportunistic spirit energies, just as you do against opportunistic thieves and aggressors in your physical life. Marauding spirits can steal your energy, and they can try to harm your body and spirit.

Everything is energy vibrating at a particular rate: your actions, thoughts, feelings, body, words, environments, work, food, drink, movies, books, music, the people you spend time with, and so forth. The more you make choices that keep you in touch with healthy, high energy, the more protected you are against attacks by low energy entities. Also picture a bright ball of white light surrounding you at all times, in all places, and before going to sleep.

Your body, mind, heart, and spirit are valuable, even precious. Keep them strong and safe by nourishing them with positive, high vibration energy.

CLEANSING THE DAY

No matter how clean your habits are, over the course of a day your body becomes dirty. Car exhaust fumes, cigarette smoke, and industrial emissions pollute the air you breathe and adhere to your skin. Physical exertion or anxiety might cause you to perspire. You also come in contact with unclean surfaces.

Just as your body becomes grimy, so does the field of energy around you. Pollutants in the cosmic air, such as negative thoughts and emotions, can adhere to your psychic skin. Your own tensions, frustrations, and disappointments produce emotional sweat. You also come in contact with contentious people and adverse environments that sully your energy field.

Cleanse both your body and your energy of the day's pollution by bathing in refreshing, rejuvenating water at the end of the day. As one of the four elements, and symbolic of emotions and spirit, water is brimming with powerful energy on both physical and metaphysical levels. If you prefer showers because you don't like sitting in dirty water, take a shower. Otherwise, bathing in a tub has certain advantages. You can add Epsom salts to the water to help draw out tension and dissolve negative energy. You can also add aromatic oils such as eucalyptus, rosemary, or lavender, which help soothe skin and muscles, mind and emotions. And a tub offers you the comfort of being able to surround your body with water, so you can soak away the day from every part of you.

Assist the water by mentally picturing the day's tensions and toxins being released into the water. Imagine that as the dirty water goes down the drain, so does the day's pollution. Bathing at night makes you clean and bright for sleeping and dreaming, which makes you fresh for the next day.

PREPARE FOR CHANGE

CYCLES of beginnings and endings are constantly taking place. An inhaled breath easily turns into an exhalation, which then makes way for the next inhalation. Day becomes night, which again transforms into day. Life, too, begins, ends, and transforms into life again, in one form or another.

Next to birth, death is the most significant event of your life. It is vitally important to prepare for it physically and spiritually. Doing so takes courage because it requires focusing on an event that you might fear. But preparing for death will strengthen you, ease your fears, and increase your appreciation of life. It will also increase your motivation to create a fulfilling life.

Prepare physically by talking with someone you are close to about what you want when you are dying. Do you want to die at a hospital, or at home? Under what circumstances do you want to be on life support systems? In a life-threatening crisis do you want to be resuscitated? When you are clear about what you want, advise your family, doctor, lawyer, and spiritual counselor. If appropriate, back it up by obtaining a Living Will. Also draw up an estate will.

To prepare emotionally, write your obituary. In addition to the events you have already experienced and accomplished, write down what you hope to have achieved in your personal and professional life. How do you want to be remembered? Doing this is powerful and helps you define your future.

To prepare spiritually, choose the circumstances of your death, whether slow or quick, in an accident or in your sleep, asking that the will of the Creator be done. Ask that the light, your guardian angel, and other spiritual guides be present to guide and protect you. Preparing for death prepares you for life.

EARTH CHANGES

PROPHECIES forecast dramatic earth events that could alter the contours of continents, shift weather patterns, and cause flooding, fires, famine, and pestilence. In short, life as we know it would be changed.

To paraphrase Chinese philosophy, change is the one thing you can count on. Even though the Earth is approximately 4.6 billion years old, it is still alive and growing. Because it is a planetary body, we forget that it is alive, even as our human bodies are alive. It is also conscious in the sense of being self-aware and self-determining, as we are, only its consciousness is far greater than ours.

The Earth has been changing for billions of years and will continue to do so. Without change there is no evolution and no life. In terms of the life span of the Earth, it may be only an adolescent. You bet it is going to change and grow. It is changing as you read this, which helps us change and grow. Accepting that it is the nature of nature to change brings greater calm than if you resist it.

When someone close to you is experiencing change, what do you do? You know you cannot stop the change from occurring, but you want to offer them understanding and support to help make their transitions smoother. Offer the Earth the same respect and consideration. After all, from the moment you are born you are engaged in the most intimate of relationships with the Earth. You breathe her air, drink her water, eat the food she grows for you, walk upon her, use her medicines, are inspired by her, taught by her, and are held close to her. What family member or friend does more for you?

Through loving physical action, positive thoughts, and prayer, support the Earth as you would someone dear to you who is changing and growing.

DREAM LIFE

"Life could be a dream, sweetheart." The lyrics of "Sh-Boom," by the 1950s American R&B group the Chords, echo what metaphysicists have been saying for centuries. Physical reality is less real than we have been led to believe, and is in fact energy in slow motion, a giant thoughtform. Physicists second the motion, having substantiated that matter is energy shaped by gravity. The linear, Newtonian view of the universe as a cause and effect, machinelike apparatus, has been replaced by the view that the universe is a grand thought.

Tune your spiritual harmony by looking at your life as if it were a dream. See the people, actions, and objects in your conscious life as being symbolic of your inner life, just as they would be in a sleeping dream. In a column, using just one or two words, list the key people in your life, activities you regularly engage in, your work, mode of transportation, and your home. Next to each entry write adjectives that describe the qualities that are most noteworthy.

Read over what you have written to see what patterns are revealed. Are the adjectives mostly positive or mostly negative? The people in your life can represent different facets of yourself. Do you recognize their primary qualities as your own? Actions show how you express your energy consciously. Do your activities limit or further you? Your car can symbolize your body, and your home your consciousness. Are they functional, for show, cramped, or roomy?

The different aspects of your material world are manifestations of your thoughts, emotions, and spirit, and as such are mirrors of yourself. If you don't like the reflection you see, change it. If you like what you see, create more of it. You have the energy. Life is a dream, so make your life a dream come true.

PERSONAL POWER

WHAT do you like to do to feel more powerful, that you did not find in *Naturally Powerful*? It could be something you do physically, mentally, emotionally, or spiritually. Write it here, describing how this positive action increases your well-being and the well-being of others, both in the present and in the future. Explain how you achieve the willingness and ability to carry it out.

GOOD QUESTIONS

How was your day? Did it enliven you, or are you glad just to have survived it? Did you learn? Did you love? These are key questions to ask yourself at the end of the day to gain perspective and help make the most of your life.

Some metaphysicists say the Creator bestows the gift of life, but you are allowed to choose the package it comes in. If that is the case, by merely surviving life you are doing it, yourself, and the Creator an immense disservice. Spending a day waiting for it to end is like being given the exact model car you want, and sitting in it in a parking space with the engine running, but not going anywhere. Or being given a stereo system and an extensive music collection, but only listening to one station on the radio. You are the driver behind the wheel of your life, take it to fascinating places. Listen to the symphony of life, feel the rhythm of jazz, blues, rock and roll, and classical music. Live each moment. Be grateful.

What gifts of learning did the day offer you? Did a mistake teach you how not to do something, bringing you a step closer to doing it successfully? Did someone show you a more efficient way of doing something, or inspire you with compassion? Did you read or hear information that confirmed or articulated something you had been considering, or did the information open a window on a new view? Acknowledge each lesson you learned, and take it to heart.

Did you love today? Did you love another, yourself, an animal, an angel, the Creator? Did you love a moment of your work? Did you love the sunset, a flower, the Earth? How did you let them know? Did you learn to love more and better? Feeling and expressing love even once each day keeps you truly alive.

Considering the day behind you, prepares you for the day ahead.

GRATITUDE ATTITUDE

HAVE you ever done something for someone—whether it was holding open a door or buying them dinner—and they didn't thank you? How did their lack of gratitude effect you? Did you feel more distant? More closed?

Do you neglect to thank others, yourself, the Creator and your higher forces for opening doors for you and nourishing you, whether physically or spiritually? Not expressing gratitude can cause these relationships to close, leaving little room for success and blessings to pass through into your life.

Expressing gratitude opens many doors. It widens the path for success, connects you with yourself and the Creator, and increases peace, health, and joy. The Balinese have specific rituals for giving thanks and give thanks many times a day for everything. They are known as being an especially peaceful and happy people, and for having an abundance of what they need.

Make an attitude of gratitude part of your everyday consciousness. Give thanks for: love, life, light, air, water, food, clothes, emotions, ideas, your body, family, friends, teachers, pets, home, job, skills, laughter, success, money, lessons, the Creator, the Earth, birds, butterflies, angels, flowers, and so forth.

Think grateful! Feel grateful! Be grateful! Write thank you notes to others, yourself, the Creator, and your guardian angel. Say "thank you" aloud. Draw or construct a large tree on a wall, then from its branches paste or hang leaves on which you've written things for which you're thankful. Light a long burning white or brightly colored gratitude candle when you've achieved a hard won success.

The principle is simple: The more you give thanks for what you have, the more you'll have to be thankful for.

HAPPY ENDINGS

On this physical plane of duality, endings are as much a part of life as beginnings. Days, nights, work, homes, letters, songs, books, touches, thoughts, feelings, flowers, seasons, years, suns, breaths, and life itself, begin and end.

An ending has to occur before a beginning can begin; you have to say good-bye before you can say hello. The quality of an ending influences the quality of the following beginning. If you say good-bye to someone in anger, then that tense, sharp energy carries into the next time you say hello to them. When you say good-bye with goodwill, the next greeting will be warm.

When an ending is accompanied by pain, such as the end of a job or a relationship, the tendency is to rush through the experience to avoid feeling the pain. This does not work in the long run. One of the best ways to avoid feeling pain later, is to feel it now. Grieve for the loss as it is happening. You are entitled. If possible, grieve for the loss with another person who is involved in it.

Endings, both fortunate and unfortunate ones, end better when you are fully present with them. To heighten awareness, ask yourself, "What needs to be healed?" Even a positive ending may have had some missteps along the way. Does a misunderstanding need to be corrected? Did you act abruptly or selfishly? Did someone else? Were your feelings hurt? Did you hurt someone? Identify these events and heal them through conversation and prayer.

Another key question is, "What did I learn?" What do you know about yourself, other people, these kinds of situations, and how the world works, that you didn't know before? What have you learned how to do, or do better? How will you use these gifts in the future? Happy endings create happy beginnings.

GREETING THE NIGHT

BEGINNINGS and endings occur in a continuum; one invariably leads to the other. One breath ends, another begins. Honoring beginnings and endings helps you empower the events that follow.

Here is a fine way to lay the day to rest and begin the night. Find a few quiet minutes alone, perhaps while bathing, or just before falling asleep. Review the events of the day. If you made mistakes, forgive yourself. See what you can learn from them, remembering that mistakes are stepping stones to growth and success. Commend yourself for having been willing to take risks. If others made mistakes, forgive them. They, too, are doing the best they are capable of.

Review the positive and enjoyable events, feelings, and ideas. Be thankful for love, laughter, opportunities, inspiration, calm moments, helpful people, and for arriving home safely. Put away the day.

Focus on the night ahead. If parts of your body need to heal, picture them receiving the positive energy they need during the night, and picture being healthier when you awake. If you have been struggling with a problem in your life, tell yourself that pertinent information to help solve the problem will come to you clearly in a dream, and that you will be able to remember the dream when you wake up in the morning. If you have been sad, angry, or frightened, ask your higher self to help you release and soothe your emotions while you sleep. If your dream spirit has something to learn, or can be of help to others while your body rests, ask for it to be guided to do so in love and light.

Ask your Creator to hold you safely in the light, all through the night, and that you awaken with delight.

BIBLIOGRAPHY

Anderson, Mary, *Colour Healing*. New York: Samuel Weiser, 1980.

Andrews, Lynn V., *Windhorse Woman*. New York: Warner Books, 1990.

Assagioli, Roberto, *The Act of Will*. Middlesex, England: Penguin, 1979.

Bandler, Richard, & John Grindler, *Frogs into Princes: Neuro Linguistic Programming*. Moab, UT: Real People Press, 1981.

Barks, Coleman, & John Moyne, *Open Secret, Versions of Rumi*. Putney, VT: Threshold Books, 1984.

Blake, William, *Songs of Innocence and of Experience*. New York: Oxford University Press, 1989.

Bly, Robert, *The Kabir Book*. Boston: Beacon Press, 1993.

Boyd, Douglas, *Mad Bear*. New York: Simon and Schuster, 1994.

——*Rolling Thunder*. New York: Dell Publishing, 1989.

Brinkley, Dannion, *Saved by the Light*. New York: Harper Paperbacks, 1995.

Brody, Harry, *Fields*. Memphis, TN: Ion Books, 1987.

Burnham, Sophy, *A Book of Angels*. New York: Ballantine Books, 1992.

Butler, W. E., *How to Read the Aura*. New York: Samuel Weiser, Inc. 1971.

Buzan, Tony, *Use Both Sides of Your Brain*. New York: E. P. Dutton, 1991.

Cameron, Julia, *The Artist's Way*. New York: G. P. Putnam's / Tarcher, 1992.

Carter, Mildred, *Body Reflexology*. West Nyack, NY: Parker Publishing Co., 1983.

Castaneda, Carlos, *Journey to Ixtlan*. New York: Simon and Schuster, 1992.

————*Tales of Power*. New York: Pocket Books, 1992.

Chopra, Deepak, *Quantum Healing*. New York: Bantam Books, 1990.

Clark, Ronald W., *Einstein: The Life and Times*. New York: Avon Books, 1994.

Cummings, E. E., *Fairy Tales*. New York: Harcourt, Brace & World, Inc., 1965.

Daniel, Almal, Wyllie Timothy, & Ramer Andrew, *Ask Your Angels*. New York: Ballantine Books, 1992.

Dass, Baba Ram, *Be Here Now*. New York: Crown Publishing, 1971.

Drake, Michael, *The Shamanic Drum: A Guide to Sacred Drumming*. Goldendale, WA: Talking Drum Publications, 1991.

Edwards, Betty, *Drawing on the Right Side of the Brain*. Los Angeles: J. P. Tarcher, Inc., 1989.

Fischer, Louis, *The Essential Gandhi*. New York: Vintage Books, 1983.

Freeman, Ira M., *Physics Made Simple*. New York: Doubleday, 1990.

Goldsworthy, Andy, *A Collaboration with Nature*. New York: Harry N. Abrams, 1990.

Hanh, Thich Nhat, *The Blooming of a Lotus*. Boston: Beacon Press, 1993.

————*The Sun in My Heart*. Berkley, CA: Parallax Press, 1988.

Hawking, Stephen M., *A Brief History of Time*. New York: Bantam, 1988.

Hoff, Benjamin, *The Tao of Pooh*. Middlesex, England: Penguin Books, 1983.

Ingerman, Sandra, *Soul Retrieval*. San Francisco: Harper Collins, 1991.

Jaworski, Joseph, *Synchronicity*. San Francisco: Berrett-Koehler Publishers, 1996.

Judson, Sylvia Shaw, *The Quiet Eye*. Washington, D.C.: Regnery Gateway, 1982.

Jung, C. G., *Memories, Dreams, Reflections*. New York: Vintage, 1965.

Lao-tzu, translated by Witter Bynner, *The Way of Life*. New York: New American Library, 1992.

Leadbeater, C. W., *The Chakras*. Wheaton, IL: Quest Books, 1972.

Liberman, Jacob, *Light: Medicine of the Future*. Santa Fe, NM: Bear & Co. Publishing, 1991.

Long, Max Freedom, *The Secret Science Behind Miracles*. Marina del Ray, CA: DeVorss Publications, 1991.

Maltz, Maxwell, *Psycho-Cybernetics*. North Hollywood, CA: Wilshire Book Co., 1981.

Maurey, Eugene, *Power of Thought*. Chicago: Midwest Books, 1990.

May, Rollo, *The Courage to Create*. New York: W. W. Norton & Co., 1994.

Murphy, Joseph, *The Power of Your Subconscious Mind*. New York: Bantam Books, 1988.

Ouseley, S. G. J., *Colour Meditations*. Alpharetta, GA: Ariel Press, 1981.

Paris, Reine-Marie, translated by Liliane Emery Tuck, *Camille: The Life of Camille Claudel*. New York: Little Brown & Company, 1984.

Peale, Norman Vincent, *The Power of Positive Thinking*. New York: Fawcett Crest, 1991.

Peterson, Scott, *Native American Prophecies*. New York: Paragon House, 1990.

Ponce, Charles, *Kabbalah*. San Francisco: Quest Books, 1973.

Progoff, Ira, *Jung, Synchronicity, and Human Destiny*. New York: Dell, 1975.

Puharich, Andrija, *Beyond Telepathy*. Garden City, NY: Anchor Books, 1973.

Raphaell, Katrina, *Crystal Enlightenment*. New York: Samuel Weiser, 1985.

Ray, Sondra, *Loving Relationships*. Berkeley, CA: Celestial Arts, 1980.

Rilke, Rainer Maria, *Rilke on Love and Other Difficulties*. New York: W. W. Norton & Co., Inc., 1994.

Roberts, Jane, *The Oversoul Seven Trilogy*. San Rafael, CA: Amber-Allen Publishing, 1995.

Rossbach, Sarah, *Interior Design with Feng Shui*. New York, NY: Arkana, 1987.

Rudel, Jean, *Panorama of the Arts*. Paris, France: Leon Amiel, 1971.

Sagan, Carl, *The Dragons of Eden*. New York: Ballantine Books, 1989.

Sams, Jamie & David Carson, *Medicine Cards: The Discovery of Power Through the Ways of Animals*. Santa Fe, NM: Bear & Co., 1988.

St. Clair, David, *David St. Clair's Lessons in Instant ESP*. New York: Signet 1991.

Schoeps, Hans-Joachim, *The Religions of Mankind*. New York: Doubleday, 1966.

Shorr, Joseph E., *Go See the Movie in Your Mind*. New York: Popular Library, 1977.

Siegel, Bernie, *Love, Medicine & Miracles*. New York: Harper & Row, 1990.

Simonton, Carl O., *Getting Well Again*. New York: Bantam, 1992.

Storm, Hyemeyohsts, *Seven Arrows*. New York: Ballantine Books, 1985.

Toben, Bob, *Space-Time and Beyond*. New York: E. P. Dutton, 1982.

Wattles, Wallace D., *Financial Success Through Creative Thought*. Holyoke, MA: Elizabeth Towne Co., 1965.

Yogananda, Paramahansa, *Autobiography of a Yogi*. Los Angeles: Self-Realization Fellowship, 1993.

Zukav, Gary, *The Dancing Wu Li Masters*. New York: Bantam Books, 1994.